Work,
Nights Out
and Other Short Stories.
by BEN TEELEY

Funny, Sad, and Everything in Between.

Getting a job, having fun in a job, avoiding trouble, having a night out and doing it all again…..and again.

PREFACE

A collection of short stories as I remember them. Others who were there might have a different memory. The journey to these stories is a simple one, I am writing them down before I forget. Changing only the names.

Living in the North East of England, leaving school, starting a job. The Sex Pistols were in their pomp, the story carries on up to when the Spice Girls were singing and dancing. Being young was fun, so was working.

Sing the songs, tell the jokes, make your customers smile, make your boss and colleagues smile, above all else, make yourself smile. I did, and hopefully some of my escapades make you smile, laugh, and perhaps even cry. The main thing is just like work, you have to stay to the end.

Thank you to my wonderful wife, without whom none of this would be possible, allowing me the time and space to complete this.

Thank you to my daughter, the structure came from you.

Thank you to Andy for your support, reviews, help and stuff.

Thank you, Gerard, for anecdotes and edits.

Thank you to everyone who ever worked with me.

And thank you Dan, you said it, I did it.

© 2022.

Cover design: nabinkarna via fiverr.com

1. **TESTING AND FITNESS**

My very first career interview was with the Royal Air Force (RAF). You would have laughed if you had seen me. I was fifteen, and a very puny looking fifteen at that. To me, a close shave was still not being caught smoking in the garden shed by my parents.

To join the RAF, you had to pass a series of written and mathematical tests. The technical jobs required a more educated calibre of candidate than if I were to join a physical fighting unit, such as the army. Amazingly, I passed all the tests.

You may not think that's much of an achievement, but in my world at that same time, I was taking nine exams at school to determine how well I had been a student at school, or was it to determine how well I had been taught? Either way, later that summer I would discover that I hadn't passed any of the nine exams at school. In fact, "hadn't passed" might be too generous a phrase, looking back at the results you could question if I had even bothered to turn up for the exams!

After I had passed the written test, I had to pass the physical examination. This is equally as important as the written tests and interviews. Many people have been declined entry into the armed forces due to a physical ailment. The medical examiner assigned to the testing was an elderly gentleman.

I can't imagine the job of medically testing skinny fifteen-year-old potential recruits is high on the list of ambitions for medics in the armed forces, and on this day, the experienced medic was wondering whose cat he had kicked to end up with me in front of him. There I stood before him, stripped to my underwear, wearing my Y-fronts that Mr. Bean would be proud of, and a physique to make Mr. Bean appear muscular.

I sat on the bed, chicken legs dangling over the edge, the medic taps my ankles, taps my knees, as soon as his little hammer touches the knee my leg kicks out as if some hidden ballerina inside me had control of my reflexes. Apparently, that's a good thing, I had great reflexes, the best reflexes of all the reflexes anyone has ever seen, in fact I used to be reflexes, I know reflexes better than anybody, even some of my friends were called reflexes.

The elderly medic never spoke much, never smiled, never said what he wanted me to do next. I gathered through his hand gestures and mumbling that for the next test I would have to lay down. I lay flat on my back, on a cold plastic examination platform. I stretched out and tried to relax, not the easiest thing for a skinny fifteen-year-old lying on his back in his Y-Fronts on a padded vinyl covered gurney.

There I was, just staring at the ceiling, counting tiles, trying to relax, wondering what the next part of the testing will be, and suddenly out of the blue, without a word the medic decides to test the reflexes of my abdomen. Well, that worked a treat, he couldn't have been more scared if someone jumped out from under the bed and grabbed his nuts from behind shouting in his ear, "Surprise!"

To say I'm a little sensitive when touched is a bit of an understatement, I burst out screaming with laughter as soon as he touched me, the silent observer must have thought my reflexes were superb, I couldn't have reacted or leapt any higher if you had made a sneak attack on my nether regions with a cattle prod. He really didn't need to touch me; I could have told him I'm the most ticklish person on the planet.

I passed the medical, although I'm certain my file must have been marked as,

"No good for spy work! Would crack as soon as he is tickled!"

They should rename the test as a "Touchy, Tickle Test!"

2. THE INTERVIEW

The final interview was in front of a panel of three to five RAF officers, to be held two weeks later, at Middlesbrough twenty-four miles south of where I lived. To get there, my journey would be in two parts, I would need to take a bus to Hartlepool covering the first eight miles, and the remainder of the journey on the train to Middlesbrough.

The RAF provided me with the appropriate travel passes. The bus would depart from close to my house around 6:30 a.m. for a thirty-minute journey, and the train would leave the station around 7:30 a.m., and take about another thirty-minutes. Once at Middlesbrough it was a twenty-minute walk to the recruitment office. With this timetable, I should easily be there by 9 a.m.

There was a problem though, the same week that the interview was scheduled, my parents would be away on holiday. For a responsible person, this is not a challenge at all. For me, I suddenly had a huge problem. I had never been much of a morning person and punctuality wasn't my style. Getting to school for 9 a.m. usually meant being rolled out of bed at 8:30 a.m. and scrambling to get ready, making it into morning assembly fifteen minutes late.

I had never seen the little hand hit the 6 o'clock twice in the same day! This would be a day that you could genuinely say would change the course of my life forever, which is a pretty big thing at fifteen. Looking back, I didn't even have an alarm clock, and if I did, I would have ignored it for sure if it went off.

I had a cunning plan, the sensible thing to do with my parents away was to enlist the help of my best friend and neighbour Keith. He and I would stay up all night together, we had done that loads of times on Fridays and Saturdays, so it made complete sense. The part I hadn't factored in was usually at 5 or 6 a.m., we would normally fall asleep and not wake up again until 2 p.m.

The first part went off without a hitch. Playing music and chatting all night was easy. Keith went back to his house at 6 a.m. and presumably to bed. I got ready and walked to the bus stop. I got on the bus, a double decker, and promptly went upstairs so I could have a cigarette. The next thing I remember is opening my eyes, the side of my head slumped against the window. As my eyes began to open and to focus, I lifted my head up, I noticed the bus had made it to the bus station.

The bus was empty. I did notice that the bus station was full. The driver had obviously pulled into his stop, dropped everyone off, then parked the bus in the wide-open space opposite the six or seven bus stands, with me asleep in the upstairs window. There must have been over a 100 people in the bus stands waiting for their buses at that time in the morning. From their position, they could quite clearly see me fast asleep with my head slumped against the window. They had all been taking bets on how long I would remain asleep. Then the worst part happened, as I was waking up lifting my head and looking around, they all started cheering and applauding!

"Oh, shit!" I thought out loud, that's not good, I hadn't even remembered falling asleep, let alone been able to fight it off.

Never mind, at least I hadn't missed the train yet. All I could do was shrug it off and get around the corner to the train station. Smiling and waving at everyone as I disembarked the bus.

Getting on the train wasn't a problem, the seats were almost full. I was only going a couple of stops, about thirty-one minutes away. Luckily, I managed to find a spot next to a nice-looking young lady and began chatting about my upcoming interview. She was not much older than I was, however, to me, she still looked much more grown up and older compared to my schoolboy looks.

The thing with commuter trains is that strangers get used to sitting beside each other. I'm not too sure how often people fall asleep on each other. As far as I can remember, the lady was very polite. When we got to Middlesbrough station she nudged me awake, and in a very polite way woke me up.

I had fallen asleep again and this time kind of slumped my head on to her shoulder. I must have looked comatose, because she didn't wake me up until the station, and she certainly seemed sympathetic to me, wanting to be sure that I was okay.

Not to be deterred, I sloped off the train and headed to the recruitment office. Once I was on my feet and in the fresh air, I would be fine. A beautiful English summer morning. The sun was just beginning to warm up the streets, it was around 8:30 a.m., I briskly walked to the recruitment office. Like a hungry Hobbit, stomach grumbling, I hadn't had any breakfast, stumbling around and looking at street signs, comparing them to my miniature map and directions provided to me by the RAF.

I found the office and proudly walked in, gave my name to the front desk officer, showed them my credentials, and glanced at the clock. I had made it, and the time was only 8:45 a.m. If Keith had been there, I could have kissed him for helping to get me there in perfect time for my panel interview.

This was it; this was the big one. Pass this and I get the approval to join the RAF, just like my father and uncle had done many years earlier. My father had been an air force mechanic and my uncle had flown over 200 missions in the second World War. Time to make the family proud.

The recruiting officer at the front desk pointed to the seats behind me and asked me to take a seat and wait until I was called. I pumped my twenty-eight-inch chest out and turned towards the chairs.

I really should have stood and waited. The chairs were positioned in the window space with their backs to the windows. The big twelve foot, clean as a whistle windows were East facing. Those of you who did considerably better than I did in exams will know that the sun rises in the East. I remember taking the seat, stretching my legs, sitting back, and enjoying how wonderful the hot sun felt on the back of my neck.

The next thing I remember is hearing voices, then the desk officer nudging me,

"Mr. Teeley! Hello Ben Teeley! They're ready for you in the interview now!"

"Huh!" I said, startled as the duty officer woke me from my slumber as I sat in the window seat.

I'd nodded off again, the poor officer had to nudge me awake to let me know that it was my turn to go into the interview room.

I went towards the room, walked through the door, and struggled to focus in the dim light, though more likely it was my eyes that were dim!

In front of me on the left-hand side of the room, sat three or four RAF officers behind an elevated long desk. Opposite the officers was a lone chair, which I headed towards. Sadly, that is all I can remember, perhaps one of them was a woman, and there may have been five of them.

For the life of me, even as I walked out, I could never remember a single thing about any of the conversations in that room. It didn't take long for the letter to land informing me that I hadn't been successful in my interview for entry into the RAF.

Can you imagine, with me on guard duty, there would be a free for all with anyone and everyone entering and leaving the camp, stealing supplies and planes as they wished.

3. JOURNEY HOME AND FIRST JOB

For many, that's where this little story would finish, for those of you good at keeping up with things, you will have realized that I haven't made it home yet. Yes, now the reverse journey was beginning. I walked back to the train station pausing only at a small shop to buy a Snickers bar.

The train station was quiet now, rush hour was over, plus we were going the other way. I got onto the train and I had a seat all to myself. Once again only travelling a few stops, Middlesbrough to Hartlepool, about thirty-one minutes.

I still had official travel passes, ensuring I wouldn't have to pay for anything. This was a good thing as I didn't have any money, beyond the small change I'd used to buy the Snickers bar. The weather was still hot, no air conditioning on the train, and I woke up, just as the train was pulling out of Hartlepool train station, the station at which I was supposed to get off and get the bus back to my home town.

At least this time I hadn't fallen asleep on a person, but I must've looked like one of those noddy dogs as my head bobbed up and down sleeping and waking, sleeping and waking, only to be asleep when I most needed to be awake at the station.

I stood up as the train continued on and somehow, I managed to stay awake until the next stop, which would be a small local line station at Seaham Harbour. Ironically, the train's route to the next station saw it trundle past my hometown, but there was no stop at my hometown. The Seaham Harbour station was about seven miles north of where I lived.

I got off the train, not sure of which way I was supposed to go. I knew I had never seen a bus go there from my hometown, so I started walking. I had no money, and my bus passes were of no use on this route.

The walk was uneventful, at least I wasn't falling asleep. I made it two or three miles when I found a road which had a bus route I knew existed and I should be able to get a bus to my hometown. I got to a bus stop and waited. Thankfully, buses ran every nine minutes. I was awake as a bus came, I started trying to explain to the driver why I had no money, only passes, and everything that had gone wrong. He laughed and told me he would let me off with the fare this time. A great guy, he even made sure I got off as close to my house as his bus route would allow. I don't remember much else from that day, except perhaps sleep.

I never did get the job in the Royal Airforce, at least I was in that rare position of not being offered a job and knowing exactly why I wasn't getting the offer. And so, without much ceremony and with only one interview, zero medicals and no written test, at sixteen years old, I landed my first job at a department store, a massive grocery, clothing, and furniture store which employed over 200 people, Fine Fare.

I still remember my very first day on the shop floor. I was asked to clean up the "Egg Cages."

These were the cages with wheels on housing the eggs that customers would buy and were easy to move on and off the sales floor when almost empty. The empty or partial empty cages were always cleaned ready to be filled again. Simple enough job you would think, except that as I rolled the first cage away I was greeted by the sight of 1000's of maggots on the bottom shelf and on floor around, luckily I didn't scream, but I'm definitely not a fisherman, and it's a day forever etched in my mind every time I go shopping, my first working day, in a supermarket, bleaching and scooping up maggots out of the egg cage.

Hooray, I was working in a place where people couldn't even check the dates on egg cartons, though as you'll see maybe that's why I fit right in ha-ha.

4. DONKEY GOES BOOM!

Sadly, we were living in the time where bomb threats were sometimes dialled into large retail businesses to cause panic and disruption. Difficult to try and explain to folks nowadays, we all knew there was very little chance that any terrorist organization would target where we lived, which meant our fear levels weren't very high, and there weren't any kind of recognised procedures in place where we lived.

In our small northern town, we were hardly at the epicentre of any political turmoil and as far as I am aware there were zero revolutionary figures in our midst who would change the face of the British government, and I'm certain nobody could have been intimidated by me and Jimmy walking through the town centre at lunchtime shouting,

"Power to the people!"

As we imitated the popular BBC sitcom of the time starring Robert Lindsay in "Citizen Smith."

When I was at school and there was a bomb threat, we would just be told to evacuate the school and sometime later army experts would descend. As far as I'm aware, every single bomb threat that the school had received, had been determined a hoax by some upset pupil. (The bomb threat posed by "Ronnie" in my book "Ben's School Days," was never reported ha-ha). Usually when a bomb threat was made to the school, we would all either be sent across the field, or we would all be sent home.

This bomb threat was my first experience of a threat happening to a business. The management didn't want to close the store for a long period of time, so as the message went out over the store tannoy system asking the customers to leave, the managers grouped the loyal, lowly employees together to explain the next steps in the store's bomb threat procedures. This was something I hadn't seen mentioned in the "Employee Handbook," or on the canteen wall along with other health and safety laws and regulations.

The management urged us not to panic, which was a good thing, because I was about to run around all hysterical and start screaming,

"Don't panic! Don't panic!"

The managers outlined the seriousness of such a situation,

"Right, we've had a bomb threat, and we need to quickly check the store for all suspicious packages. You four lads will go and check the warehouse, while we check the salesfloor!"

Ah, so all we had to do was to go and check the warehouse for bombs! Cool, I was being paid about £15 a week, yes around 40p per hour, and most of my colleagues made the same amount of money. Obviously, such a princely sum made us what you might call, "expendable." Preferable to risk one if us than just allow a bomb to mash some of the potatoes in the warehouse.

"Okay!" we said, "Let's go looking for a bomb!"

Four of us started walking slowly towards the warehouse, me, Jimmy, Benny, and Donkey. We glanced behind us noticing that the managers were remaining congregated around the checkout supervisor's office, laughing, and joking. In those days ninety percent of the checkout operators were female, and ninety percent of our managers were male.

"Hmmm, we're going looking for a bomb while they stand flirting with each other!" I exclaimed to Jim.

"Well it's no surprise, isn't it not, I mean one of us is already nicknamed "Donkey!" Jim replied in his normal double negative way of speaking, while laughing.

Donkey came by his nickname honestly, apart from his lack of intellectual acumen, he always worked hard, and he was great at pushing shopping carts. I'm not so sure this qualified Donkey to be at the forefront of a bomb search unless we could all hide behind him.

As my gallant colleagues and I walked towards the warehouse, we began to put aside our thoughts of the managers and the checkout girls and focus on the task in front of us.

"Never mind them, we will be the important ones." I said.

"Yeah," agreed Jim, "We will be saving the shop!"

We puffed our twenty-eight-inch chests out and started to walk like the Bruce Willis team in "Armageddon."

"Yeah, them checkout lasses will arl be fancying us instead!" Chimed in Benny.

We would be the heroes; they would make Avengers movies about us thirty years before Avengers' movies were made but wait!

We had questions.

Donkey asked, "Does anyone know what a bomb looks like?

"Not really," replied Benny, "but I bet it would stand out from our other stuff! I mean more important is where would you put a bomb in a warehouse?"

Jim laughed and said, "Well it might be disguised in cans of beans for all we know! Mightn't it?"

Now I was laughing, albeit a little nervously, and asked "Would you really want to disrupt the Heinz beans supply to small town England? I mean what would we put on our toast if the beans were all blown up?"

"Ha-ha!" Benny laughed, "Can you imagine the mess with potatoes and cans of beans flung everywhere?"

"Ha-ha, yeah!" Donkey joined in, "We could all just get out a fork and there's lunch sorted!"

We were all laughing at the thought of Donkey sat in the middle of a warehouse explosion with his fork eating the potatoes and beans all around him. Not much of a political statement would be being made if that was on the national news.

Imagine the six O'clock news, "Today, at a supermarket in the north, there was an explosion in the warehouse. We go now live to Billy Broadcaster who is in the warehouse, as we watch Donkey begin the clearing up process. Over to you Bill!"

"Hello, I'm here, live in the warehouse where you can see the damage, and over there the clean-up operation is beginning!"

"Bill, what is that we see in the middle of the warehouse?"

"Oh, that's Donkey, he decided the best thing to do was to eat his way through the potato and beans explosion, as he said when we interviewed him, "Waste not, want not! Now, back to you in the studio."

"Thank you Billy, we will continue to bring you updates from this story as Donkey eats his way through the devastation left by the beans and potato bomber!"

We carried on laughing and walked through the warehouse doors, they swung closed behind us, yet another reminder of our expendability rating, the doors would shield the managers from any damage to us and the potatoes.

We looked around at each other, the four of us aged sixteen to eighteen, thoughts of our own mortality began to permeate the air.

Not only did we possess zero knowledge of bombs or have any experience in a uniformed service beyond the boy scouts, but I'm also quite sure there were two of us who couldn't even spell bomb or change a plug.

Yet here we were, about to be climbing shelving and looking under fixtures for bombs.

"So, Jim," I said, "What will we do if we find a bomb?"

"Run fast!" Said Jim laughing.

"Right then, maybe we should split up, at least we will be able to search quicker, and only one of us goes boom!"

"Aye okay then!" Said Benny, as we each headed for the four corners of the warehouse.

I seem to remember after about thirty seconds, we all worked out that we didn't want to be the expendable type, we weren't Avengers, not brave, and at such an early age we learned the truth behind the saying,

"Discretion is the better part of valour!"

None of us was looking too hard to try and find "a bomb."

After five minutes, I shouted "Hey lads!" I was sat on top of an industrial fridge across the warehouse, "Here on top of this fridge!"

They quickly came running, all excited, Jim the first to get to the bottom of the step ladder I had used, looked up grinning and said,

"You haven't found a bomb, haven't you not!"

The other two were just a step behind him, "Well?" They asked in unison.

"Nah!" I said, "But I have found where they hide the broken chocolate from the shop floor!"

There the four of us sat and consumed broken bars of chocolate, laughing like Andy Dufresne and his prison gang on the sunny roof in "Shawshank Redemption" after he had bargained for them to have some suds to drink. We didn't regard this as stealing, firstly we were maybe having our last meal if there was a bomb, and secondly, this is the stuff they threw away and was often shared by management and staff, oh how times have changed.

After a while, the management must have decided that there wasn't any bomb and the "all clear" was announced over the tannoy system. Down the step ladder we scurried and decided that we should re-enter the shop area at separate intervals so it didn't look like we had all just hung out in the warehouse, like we had.

Even though we understood that most of these bomb warnings were from weirdos just causing trouble, I would still love to go back in time, question the managers, and ownership, regarding the sanity of a company sending its most junior staff to look for bombs!

Imagine if we had found one. I can see it now, Donkey holding up a package of cornflakes with wires sticking out one end, an alarm clock taped to the front, sticking out from the other end a big red stick with the cartoon letters "Bomb" clearly visible. Donkey's last words,

"What the fuck's this?"

We could have all gone boom and to add insult to injury we weren't even provided with a set of pliers, body armour, a fancy hat, or a flashlight.

I'm sure that must be somewhere in the store handbook of how to look for bombs, maybe on page ninety-nine of the safety regulations.

5. **BENNY AND HIS MESS**

Jimmy and I played pranks on the other lads and lasses around our age and work group, us against them, all in fun of course, just silly pranks, things like taking a dirty mop and using it to paint the outside of a warehouse stock fridge, that had just been cleaned the day before a corporate store inspection, or kind of accidentally on purpose walking down aisles turning all the labels on the food cans the wrong way round so someone would have to go back down an aisle and face them up again, yes that was serious business, as was de-carbonizing, the made up technical term for removing cardboard. Nothing serious, just a nuisance really.

Baby-faced Benny oversaw the dairy and delicatessen fridges, milk, cream, eggs, cheese, bacon, and cooked meats. Part of his morning routine included going through all his shop floor fridges and removing out of date, damaged or "sell by" dated foods and dairy from display. We called him "baby-face," coz his face would always scrunch up with that bottom lip quiver whenever we re-arranged his shop floor cheese displays.

Some days for Benny were lighter than others. One day he might have two or three yoghurts and a couple of egg boxes, other days he would wish he had grabbed a shopping cart to make it easier to carry everything from the shop floor back through to the warehouse and dispose of it into the skip.

This particular day, Benny came through the big double doors from the shop floor to the warehouse and was walking towards the skip. Benny's arms were full, too full, he hadn't bothered with a shopping cart, and he was carrying a box full of damaged or outdated milk, yoghurts, eggs, and assorted dairy, precariously balanced. Benny had determined that instead of making a couple of trips safely, he would carry everything at once. The trouble was he could barely see over the top of the damaged and dated dairy mountain that he was carrying.

Jimmy and I were walking from the other direction towards him. This was just too good an opportunity to miss.

"Don't you not think Baby would look like he'd worked a bit harder if some of that stuff had actually splashed on his work clothes?" Asked Jimmy.

"Sure!" I replied, "and as he's carrying so much, it's not likely he's gonna make it to the skip. After all it's a messy job and carrying too much in one trip is bound to result in a mishap."

"Yeah!" Jimmy laughingly agreed, "Let's give him a hand."

Benny was almost at the skip and seeing us laughing, he immediately sensed his position of weakness.

We talked him through our plan to help him.

"You look busy!" Laughed Jimmy.

"Yeah," I chipped in, "it seems you're carrying a bit too much there Baby!"

Benny remained calm and tried a nervous smile, as he said,

"Now you two bugger off and leave me alone, I'm busy!"

"Oh, we can see you're busy!" Jim said.

"Yeah," I joined in, "We're going to help you!"

"But, but I don't need your help!" Benny said nervously, realising his faux bravado hadn't worked.

"Sure you do," Jimmy said, as he picked up a broken carton of milk, from the top of the pile.

"Damaged milk cartons are a messy thing, and you can't be too careful. Jimmy will put it in the skip for you!" I said, laughing, as Jimmy tipped a little of the milk down the front of Benny's pants before discarding the broken carton into the skip.

"See there's one done for you!" We both exclaimed! "Your load is already lighter."

"Ooh look, you have some damaged yoghurts, you have to be really careful with those, don't you Jimmy?" I said as Jimmy and I each picked one up.

Grinning, we looked at each other, nodded in agreement, Laurel and Hardy style, as we each poured one into the side pockets of his overall, also splashing a little down his trousers to add to the milky effect.

Then as we threw the little empty yoghurt cartons into the skip, we said,

"See a bit more done for you, and now you look like you have been really busy!"

Benny still had his arms full, still holding the box.

"Bastards!" He exclaimed as we took a few steps back while admiring our handy work, complementing each other, on just how helpful we were.

"Now that's no way to thank us Benny! If you'd been more careful we wouldn't have had to be so helpful." I said laughing.

"Yeah, today's training was 'why you should've used a trolley!" Jimmy said, "I mean there's only 500 to choose from ha-ha!"

Baby-faced Benny turned red, his bottom lip was up, his anger was building and about to explode, he decided to try and get even, and in one move, he dropped his cargo of damaged and out-of-date dairy junk on the floor in front of the skip, grabbing yoghurts from the top of his cargo and simultaneously launching yoghurts at me and Jimmy, who by now had retreated about four to six feet away from him.

Like a scene from the wild west, where the attacker is such a bad shot, the yoghurts whizzed past us, he had missed like a cross eyed gunslinger from all of four feet.

Unbeknown to Benny, the reason Jimmy and I had ceased to be a nuisance and stood passively and continued backing away, wasn't because we were worried about what he could do, but because at that exact moment, we had noticed the double doors Benny had come through, were now being opened and walked through by Mr. Robinson, our manager.

Mr. Robinson hadn't seen Jimmy or I anywhere near Benny, and unfortunately for Benny, he was now between ten and twenty feet away at the exact moment when Benny made the decision to drop his box and launch his surplus out of date dairy towards us, the exact moment that the outdated yoghurts were sailing by our ears.

All Mr. Robinson could see was Benny clowning around and launching his out-of-date dairy towards us. Those are the days you wish cameras and slow motion were as commonplace as today. Just as Benny is letting go, you can hear from behind him Mr. Robinson with a loud,

"Clarke, what are you doing?"

Whilst from in front, Jimmy and I were dodging yoghurts and in our most earnest and sincere voices shouting in unison,

"No! Benny please don't! We told you not to throw it at us!"

The look on Benny's face as he heard Mr. Robinson shout from behind him was priceless, you could see his body shudder as if he had just been tasered and shat his pants. No matter how many, "But, but but's," or quivering lips, as Benny tried to explain, the mess down the front of his clothes simply looked like he had just carried too much dairy.

Benny was hauled off to the human resources lady to face his punishment for attacking poor helpless Jimmy and I, and to add insult to injury, Benny was told to apologize to us. An apology which we both graciously accepted on the condition that Benny wouldn't attack us in future.

6. NUT FLICKER

Dishing out practical jokes means that you have to be prepared to accept others playing practical jokes back to you. Cliffy was one such character, always looking to embrace the humour at work, he thought it would be funny to flick me in the nuts (testicles). Though to this day, I'm still not sure of the humour involved in this particular activity.

At school, several years earlier, as told in "Ben's School Days," we had Bobby the serial nut flicker to look out for, he had gotten me once and made me literally throw up. This made me avoid any activities that would involve the possibility of other lads flicking my nuts, clearly, it's a thing for some boys.

Unfortunately, at work this day, Cliffy was in stealth mode and managed to catch me off guard. He was altogether too accurate, not only did I throw up, but I also had to go home for the rest of the day. You do have to question the wisdom and sensibility of such an activity when we were working with knives and bacon slicers, I mean there wouldn't be much laughter if I'd sliced my own right arm off!

The next day, when I returned to work, my manager, Mr. Nelly, told me I had to go to H.R. and fill in the "sick forms." I didn't think this was unusual, I hadn't been sick before, perhaps there was some special paperwork to complete.

I hadn't been back to H.R. Since the day I was hired, when I was given my name tag and new brown overall, me, Dean and Karen were the newbies that day, feeling important. Every time I had seen Mrs. Brown in passing she always seemed like a lovely lady. I went into her grand office, and sat in an oversized, expensively upholstered chair facing her huge desk. She was how I would have termed old, but at that age everyone who was older than me, would have qualified as "old!" Which really means Mrs. Brown was only in her forties.

She was sitting in an even bigger chair than the one I was in, complete with wings on the headrest, and looked tiny behind her desk, almost as if the whole set up had been comically designed for a bunch of school kids to play at being grown-ups.

Mrs. Brown smiled at me and asked,

"I see you had to go home sick yesterday, how are you feeling today?"

I shuffled nervously in my seat, smiled, and replied, "Oh, I'm much better thank you! I had a good rest and should be okay from now on."

Mrs. Brown continued, "I'm just a little concerned that you had to go home sick yesterday."

"Oh right!" I said, quickly trying to think of what exactly she had been told about me going home, my manager hadn't mentioned it to me when he sent me up to see her, and I didn't think it much of a big deal, I certainly didn't want to attract attention to the fact that if anyone touched my nuts, I would throw up. I hadn't even complained about Cliffy, and I don't know who had, after all he was one of my mates and I was sure he was just trying to be funny. I had thought to just move on and carry on back to normal.

However, Mrs. Brown was treating this issue very seriously.

She leaned forward in her chair, almost to an interrogating pose and asked, "So where did this happen?"

Now I could feel the spotlight on me, I was beginning to feel flushed in the face. I was a young sixteen, feeling under pressure to answer without getting anyone in trouble. I completely misunderstood the intent of her question and started to squirm in my oversized seat.

Mrs. Brown was adamant, "I need to know this for your records!"

She seemed oblivious that this young teenage boy was starting to sweat, the room was looking blurry to me, I definitely wasn't comfortable discussing my testicles and here she was pressing the point. At that time of life, I hadn't even sworn in front of a girl, except for the one time I said, "F-off!" As told in Ben's Schooldays, never mind talked about my testicles. All the adults I knew didn't even acknowledge the existence of a young man's testicles.

Within milliseconds, questions were flying through my head,

"What words would I use?"

"Do I use adult medical terminology?"

"Can I even think of adult medical terminology?"

As far as my world went, all the lads called their testicles, balls, nuts, goolies or knackers! None of these words seemed appropriate as I felt myself getting all hot under the collar, going bright crimson as the blood rushed to my head, losing eye contact with her and kind of shuffling in my seat.

My brain decided that it would be better not to say the words, better to behave as Mr. Bean would and try to make her see through an elaborate use of hand gestures. While still shuffling uncomfortable in my large seat, I raised my right arm so it was visible above the desk from where she sat, I curved my hand, extending my index finger as I pointed downwards to where the middle of the top of my legs were and said,

"Down there, the right one!"

Mrs. Brown burst out laughing, and she continued laughing for a month after that! Through the tears of her laughter she said,

"No, no! Not that! Oh ha-ha, I mean where abouts in the shop did it happen. Was it in your lunch hour or was it on work time?"

"Oh I see!" I blurted out, the penny finally dropping for me.

Suddenly feeling that I had just negotiated the deadliest curve on a perilous mountain racing course and elated that we weren't going to be talking about my testicles. Even better, with the last part of her sentence, I now also knew the basis for any procedures against Cliffy.

If I said it was at work in the preparation room and on the work clock, he was in trouble, though I'm sure after laughing so hard Mrs. Brown would have found it difficult to hand out any kind of punishment.

What would have been excellent would have been the opportunity to run back down to the preparation room we worked in and ask Cliffy how much it was worth not to snitch ha-ha.

Naturally, I told her that we were outside of work and fooling around on our own time. Cliffy went free, and thankfully, that was the last time anyone flicked me in the nuts.

Though not the end of practical jokes between me, Cliffy, Jimmy and anyone else who wanted to join in.

7. FLYING EGGS

Boredom at work can only lead to problems. Me and Jimmy would get bored and be walking through the warehouse, looking for things to do, as soon as we established there were no urgent work needs, we would wonder what else we could get up to, usually our conversations would start along the lines of,

"Sure is quiet today!"

"Yup!"

"You bored?"

"Yup!"

"Do you think there's much going on in the warehouse?"

"Let's take a look and if there isn't there soon will be ha-ha!"

As we rounded the corner we saw the open door of a huge industrial fridge, at the back of the "Deli Counter," the kind with such a large noisy motor inside that even if we were stood beside each other, we would have to shout at each other to be heard. There inside working away with his back to us was Cliffy.

Giggling like ten-year old's, well we really were still kids, we decided this was a great opportunity to have a pop at Cliffy and not be caught.

"We could go get some eggs and chuck them at him and he'd never know!" We both nodded in agreement.

We quickly ran to the main storage area and found a couple of out-of-date eggs, then made our way back to the open door of the fridge.

Cliffy was still there with his back to us as Jimmy and I launched a couple of eggs towards Cliffy's back. As soon as the eggs left our hands, we turned and ran to hide behind the nearest large pallets of potatoes.

Each pallet was stacked around six feet tall, and two or three of them stacked at once, not too difficult to hide behind. The advantage of hiding behind these was you could still see through some gaps which way a person was heading and then easily move around out of his or her line of sight.

We knew Cliffy would come flying out, he had nice, freshly permed hair, popular at the time, and would be looking for revenge. Just as we made it behind the first stack, Cliffy did come flying out, oh boy! Success, ha-ha, one of us had hit the back of his overall and the other the back of his head, Jimmy and I should've been trialists for the local cricket team.

It took all of our willpower not to let the laughs out, we knew Cliffy would be mad and while he wouldn't bother me and Jimmy together, if he knew it was us he could certainly bother us individually, keeping quiet was our priority. We could joke about it later with him once he'd calmed down, and ask him,

"How was your egg shampoo?"

What we hadn't expected was that anybody else would be working in the vicinity. Poor Donkey, there he was, minding his own business, busy re-arranging pallets in the far corner of the warehouse. As Cliffy came flying out of his fridge, the first thing he noticed was Donkey.

Cliffy ran towards Donkey while screaming at him,

"I suppose you think that's funny?"

"Huh?" Was a perfectly reasonable and puzzled response from Donkey.

Not only had we not been caught, now we also had Donkey as a suspect that Cliffy was prepared to believe was responsible. Jimmy and I began to feel relieved and let a little laughter slip out.

Laughing at our own success, we came out of our hiding place to get a better view of what we thought would be Cliffy throwing eggs back at Donkey in revenge, and starting a warehouse egg fight, we could even join in and have a right old messy food fight. Although as we'd come out of hiding, we had by now noticed that Cliffy didn't have any eggs in his hands. Donkey wasn't playing along either and wasn't at all impressed that Cliffy was blaming him, Cliffy grabbed Donkey and told him in no uncertain terms he was going to pay for this.

"You better clean this off!" Yelled Cliffy!

Donkey looked back at Cliffy, tried to push him away and said,

"Fuck off!"

Oops, Cliffy didn't hesitate and without a second thought he raised his hand to slap Donkey.

Jimmy and I immediately jumped up looking to stop any physical altercation, and together shouted,

"Woah! Hey! No! It wasn't him! It was us!"

Cliffy looked across at us, with an expression as if he'd heard us but didn't want to hear us, because we were about to spoil his fun, then turned back, slapped Donkey and began the walk back to where we were.

"Oh no!" We said, "You didn't have to hit him! It was us! We didn't expect you to clobber anyone!"

Cliffy, now with a big grin on his face, said

"Ah well I don't care, I never liked him anyway!"

Oh shit! Sorry Donkey if you're reading this.

Jimmy and I would have to be a little more careful in future about who we targeted and whether we should even hide anymore, I mean after all, if anyone wanted a practical joke war, they were bound to lose against us.

8. BIG MOUTH

I was working with Cliffy; we were busy outside the same noisy industrial fridge Cliffy was in when me and Jim had thrown eggs at him, and which I had previously sat on top of eating broken chocolate with my fellow bomb hunters, we were preparing deliveries ready for storage in the huge fridge behind us. Occasionally, people walked past, mainly to and from the canteen.

As the ladies walked by, Cliffy would find great mirth in assigning them a number between one and ten based on how pretty, or how much Cliffy fancied them. Not even able to conceal his laughter at his own humour as the girls passed us by. I mean it might've been funny if Donkey had walked past and he said something like a two!

Cliffy would just say a number between one and ten of how pretty the young lady might be, and I was supposed to agree or say higher or lower. In this way, anyone passing by was to assume we were discussing our stock predicament at fitting it all into the fridge or assessing the weight of a piece of meat.

I know this is not politically correct, though karma has a strange way of working. Most of the workforce were all sweet young ladies, and through my rose-tinted eyes, most were a nine or ten anyway.

Karen and Christine would walk past and Cliffy would say,

"Seven's and eights!"

And I would reply,

"Oh more than that!"

If one of the security women or supervisors went past, Cliffy would usually be in the middle and say something like,

"Five or six maybe?"

I would decline to comment based on the lesson learned during the bomb search that "discretion is the better part of valour!" These ladies weren't stupid and it wouldn't take much to give away Cliffy's sometimes obvious indiscreet comments.

Some of the younger girls would giggle knowing fine well what we were doing, others particularly supervisors or management would be too busy to notice.

Then Joanne walked past. Joanne worked in the canteen and was a sturdy lady of no small physique and certainly not a person to be crossed, even the senior management didn't try to tell Joanne what to do in the canteen. You're probably thinking ahead, and you'd be right, Cliffy thought he had the game down to a fine art where neither he nor I would look at anyone, we knew them all already, and we certainly wouldn't mention a name or imply anything.

As Joanne walked by, Cliffy spurted out,

"Two!"

At the same time, he couldn't hide his admiration at his own humour and laughed a little. Joanne didn't even break step and as she kept moving towards Cliffy she said,

"What did you say?"

Cliffy pretended to play dumb merely saying,

"Huh?"

He didn't even have time to blink as Joanne's free hand came up and slapped across his face at the speed of light. Cliffy's cheek instantly burning red, him fuming because he didn't know how to cope with being slapped.

We never played that game again! Even the biggest butcher in the building wouldn't have tried crossing Joanne, mind you there are those that might say he was being generous with a "two."

Despite always putting his foot in his mouth, Cliffy never seemed to learn from his experiences. Always ready to laugh, the problem was he just didn't know when not to say something or when to keep it to himself.

One morning, he came running into the food preparation room from the front counter shouting at me, while laughing hysterically, that I should go out front and

"See the size of this lad's head!"

Sadly, for Cliffy, the young man in question was waiting at the end of the counter to speak to his mom. His mom was standing working beside me.

Everyone in the store except Cliffy must have known that he was born with a defect which enlarged his skull and that his mom worked there. To the mom's credit, she never got angry, she turned very calmly to Cliffy and said,

"That's my son! He was born that way."

The young man may have had an enlarged cranium, but even with his disadvantage, his mouth was never going to be as big as Cliffy's.

Oh, floor please open and swallow Cliffy.

9. **STARSKY AND HUTCH**

One of the great things about working at the oversized department store was that we had our very own Starsky and Hutch. Not the real ones of course, but the resemblance was uncanny.

One was dark haired and one fair, one was tall and handsome and the other wasn't. Both were young and ambitious, both oversaw the food area and warehouse, supply chain, storing and display of goods. Though it would be Hutch who would have the most magnificent moments of buffoonery.

Just in time for Easter the store would always receive thousands of chocolate Easter eggs. The goal was to try and get them all out onto the sales floor as soon as possible; however, occasionally you had to store some in the warehouse.

Nearly all packaged food deliveries came on pallets, stacked about six feet tall. The system wasn't complicated, pallets filled with canned goods, beans, or soups for example, could be stacked on top of each other up to three pallets high in the warehouse, saving space, which with the pallet included put the stack well over twenty feet. Quite a formidable array of food stock we had to shift onto the sales floor.

With soft goods the only way you stacked them up a height was on top of canned goods, common sense tells you that you wouldn't put soft goods on the bottom pallet and stack other goods on top. For example, a pallet of cereal may be stacked on top of two pallets of beans, but you would never stack beans on top of cereal.

I see you're thinking ahead, and you're right. Super Hutch stacked the three chocolate Easter eggs pallets one on top of the other. It only took about five minutes before the middle and bottom pallets just collapsed under the weight and the top one fell onto the floor, destroying around 1000 chocolate Easter eggs in the process. That was a good year for employees to get discounted or free broken chocolate eggs, there certainly wasn't room on top of any of the fridges for that much broken chocolate.

Super Hutch's partner, Starsky didn't fare much better when it came to driving a forklift responsibly in the warehouse. One of the worst jobs we had was to clean the warehouse floor, using big, horrible mops. We usually only did this last thing at night or Saturday afternoon; the store was closed on a Sunday.

Starsky decided that the laws of physics wouldn't apply to him and that he could drive an electric three wheeled forklift through the warehouse, the floor was still wet. As if anyone really needed an illustrated guide about how useless forklift trucks are on wet warehouse floors, Starsky decided to drive across it, illustrating to those watching with open mouths, who already knew, that the brakes don't work on a wet floor, and are even dangerous.

Once the brakes are activated, the rear wheel will lock on the wet surface, forcing the forklift to skid, continuing its momentum, no turning, no stopping, just sliding in the direction you were originally heading, which was in this case into the side of an industrial fridge unit almost destroying it.

These are the days at work when you learn that if a manager causes £1000's in damages it's funny, everyone laughs, and the insurance company will cover the damage, but if you or one of your colleagues cause damage to even one Easter egg, the result is vastly different, and not so funny anymore.

Not so much Starsky and Hutch as more like Abbott and Costello.

10. SPITTING TEETH

At sixteen years old, you expect to go to work, do your part and at the end of the day hang out with your mates. Working at a supersized department store, not much out of the ordinary ever happened. That is, not until the day I got my face smashed in by an angry truck driver.

I was working on the loading bay of the warehouse. The area where all the goods were delivered, and whether they were food, clothes or diamonds, they all came in that big rear entrance. Huge open shutters rolled up and, in the winter, you froze, while in the summer you were bugged by the flies around the rubbish skip.

The entrance was wide enough for three trucks to back into, though in reality never more than two ever came in, as the third space was occupied by the skip. The warehouse was designed so that as a lorry backed in, the open back of the lorry would be the same height as the warehouse floor. This meant that we were standing four feet above the road on a walkway between the warehouse and the sales floor about twelve feet wide.

Two of the characters I had the good fortune to work with were George and Frank.

George was the warehouse and loading bay manager. George was old fashioned and very disciplined, everybody loved George. I'm sure he should have been retired but his organisational abilities and the fact that nobody could pass George's security checks meant he was invaluable to the store. If George trained you and liked you, the senior managers knew you were a good egg. George did have a bad arm which he carried in a fixed position, I never asked why, and he never spoke about it, he was a burly fella, he always worked harder than anyone else.

Frank had been hired to lighten the load for George, so that George could be more of a supervisor and oversee more of the furniture and other non-food items. Frank had one eye, so "Frankie One Eye" wasn't a stretch for a nickname, though not to his face from a bunch of kids. Frankie was also skinny, he smoked roll up cigarettes, and was old, well he looked old to me at sixteen, I would say at least into his fifties.

Frank reported to George and I reported to Frank.

Their people skills were as different as chalk and cheese. George was always polite and respectful, George would use a swear word if he got hurt by something falling on his foot. Frank on the other hand must have had Tourette's. if you said,

"Good morning!" to Frank, the response was always along the lines of.

"Good fucking morning, ahl give yer good fucking morning. What's fucking good about it? We've fucking got tons of fucking work to fucking do and fucking not enough fucking time to fucking do it."

It was always the "f" word and he inserted it more than he breathed between puffs of his cigarette. While not allowed to smoke on the loading bay, he could easily step down and walk twenty-five feet forwards to the outside and have a quick tab while waiting for the next vehicle. This was usually only in the afternoons when things slowed down a bit. Needless to say, Frank was never going to be managing the customer service side of the business anytime soon.

Neither Frank nor I were the biggest of people and with only twelve feet of roll off space as you rolled down a ramp from the back of a lorry with the handheld forklift, you had to turn quickly or hope you would stop before being crushed against the wall. Seems madness looking back, my shadowy sixty-three kilo frame (140lbs) having the equivalent of a baby elephant slamming me into the wall. Luckily, drivers and some others would always help with huge loads.

Despite the poor pay and working conditions, this was a prestigious position, responsible for a lot of incoming goods, these stores could go through £200,000 worth of goods in a busy week. A lot of responsibility, teamwork, a great grounding for demanding 100% from those around you.

Some days were really easy, you would start at 6 a.m., well let's be honest, I didn't make it to work too often at 6 a.m. George and Frank would always be there, I used to get there around 7 a.m. or 8 a.m. Frank always complained, but I figured for fifteen quid a week, I can work from 7 a.m. or 8 a.m. until 6 p.m. Instead of 6 a.m. to 6 p.m. Without overtime.

The day in question we were busy, right from 6 a.m. I had come in early by request as we knew it was going to be a busy day. We had lorries waiting around the corner and we were working hard. Imagine a fast-food drive through nowadays, only instead of cars it's lorries, back-to-back. The lorry drivers were helping us, so we decided to focus as a team unloading one at a time.

When the hand pulled mini forklift couldn't fit on to the back of a flatbed lorry, the truck drivers, as many as six of them, would stand in a line with Frank and I as boxes of food were picked up from the pallet on the back of the lorry, passed from one to the other and stacked on an empty pallet on the loading bay.

With about eight lorries outside, this was as close to organised chaos as you would ever get.

Early in the morning, around 6 a.m. The driver of a non-food (furniture) lorry came in, he was only about five foot six inches tall, looked to be in his thirties, thick set, all aggressive and upset. He'd driven through the night, was first there, and wanted to know why he wasn't being unloaded? And when would he be unloaded?

His delivery was non-food, furniture, non-perishable, that meant to George, Frank, and anyone who cared, that he was an extremely low priority to unload. The order of the day would be, fresh fruit and vegetables first, bread, milk, frozen, dairy, fresh meats, then regular food, then he would be in the final batch, and looking at the amount we had to do, it would be sometime in the afternoon.

Of course, it had to be Frank who politely explained that morning's well-planned schedule that was in place for the day,

"Fer fuck's sake, we fuckin busy, yer just have ter fuckin wait! We'll get ter yer when we fuckin get ter yer!"

The driver seemed a little shell shocked, eventually swore back at Frank and then went back outside to his vehicle to wait.

We carried on, working as fast as we could. Once the goods were unloaded from a lorry, we had to start checking the items against the invoice which we would have to sign. Then we would have to move the stock from the loading bay into the warehouse, so the relevant department could use the stock. We kind of had a "system" and we were getting through articulated lorries, as quickly as we could.

About 9 a.m. The furniture lorry driver came back in, still upset at waiting and demanding to know how much longer he would have to wait. He wanted to get back on the road and be home for his afternoon.

Frank wasn't the very sympathetic type, and let him know,

"Ah dinnit fuckin give a fuck, how fuckin long you've fuckin been waiting. We have to fuckin, do these other fuckin loads first!"

The lorry driver was mad now. He replied something along the lines of,

"This is fucking ridiculous, I've been waiting hours now, I need to know, when you are going to unload my stuff?"

Frank responded, "We'll fuckin get ter yer, when we fuckin get ter yer, we're fuckin busy, and there's fuck arl we can fuckin dee about it!"

The pair of them started shouting at each other, while the rest of us on the loading dock kept busy unloading lorries. I remember very clearly the driver saying to Frank,

"That's it, I'm not waiting anymore, I'm taking it back!"

By now you could guess Frank's response, "Whey gan on, fuck off, I dinnit fuckin care!"

The driver jumped down from the loading bay and walked back to his lorry. We heard it start up, the driver moved it backwards and forwards a little then stopped the engine, jumped out and came back in. I was at the edge of the loading bay catching boxes from one of the drivers and passing them to the next bloke along. He didn't go up the side where the steps were, he came up where I was, pulled himself up onto the loading bay and this time was asking to see the store manager.

Frank was ignoring him, and he stood with his back to the wall watching us unload the lorry, a line of about eight of us. He seemed a little calmer and was waiting for George, who had kept appearing and disappearing, though wisely George had resisted getting involved in Frank's decision about who we would unload and when.

I thought I would be nice, give the driver some reassurance. I was catching boxes of canned food, I was in a rhythm, catching to my left and swivelling to my right to throw it to the next bloke, a system we called "handballing."

Each time I swivelled; the driver was in my line of view about eight feet away from me. I could see him standing there, and kind of felt sorry for him, especially as Frank's diplomacy hadn't exactly come from the Dale Carnegie book about winning friends.

As I'm catching a box and turning to pass it on, I kept on catching his eye, perhaps he was just glaring at employees for all I know. I decided to say something to let him know we were going to help him. All I said was,

"Don't worry, we will get to you as quickly as we can."

The last words must have exited my mouth as I was completing my turn to the right, the next thing I saw was just like in the movies.

As I turned to go back to the left for the next box, I hadn't seen him dash towards me. I did see this perfectly formed fist heading inches from my face, it was exactly like slow motion in a movie, but that's ridiculous because there it was connecting with my face. Yet I still remember clear as day, as if I were the camera lens and the fist was heading to the camera before the screen goes blank, just like in a John Wayne punch up.

I felt myself flying through the air, remember, my starting point was four feet above the ground below. This was all surreal, I met the ground with a thud. My brain still couldn't work it out, I knew I wasn't in a movie. I tried to get to my feet, my legs didn't respond to my thoughts, everything was blurry.

I felt myself being grabbed by the lapels of my work overall, it was the driver who had hit me, a man in his thirties, hitting a sixteen-year-old skinny boy, in a line of eight other truck drivers, a true coward in my book.

He had jumped down after me and now he had hold of me. I didn't know whether to try and protect my face from a possible head butt, or if he was going to knee me. I pissed myself and put my hands across my balls and tried to beg him not to hit me again.

I'm not sure if words came out because my mouth was a mess, he was shocked at the damage he had done to me, he didn't use any more violence. In a split second another warehouse manager, Mr. Jones, jumped down, and grabbed him.

While Mr. Jones held him, I swivelled around to run away, my vision was blurred, my legs were wobbly. I could see a bright light where the sun came into the entrance about twenty feet away, where the front of the lorry was. I staggered in that direction, stumbling and sobbing as I went, not able to see correctly and no clue where I was going to hide to try and save myself. I knew I wanted to hide, crawl away somewhere and sob.

Somebody else had come down the steps on the other side of the lorry and got to the front of the lorry at the same time as me. They took my hand and said it was alright to go with them back inside. I remember we walked up the other side of the lorry, up the steps and on to the top of the loading bay again. I was shaking and sobbing in shock; I do remember the store General Manager, Mr. Rollings, coming around the corner looking incredibly angry, upset, and shocked all at the same time. Somebody said call the police, and then somebody else suggested they get me to the canteen to clean me up.

We were heading to the canteen, security ladies either side of me, holding me up, helping me along. I was still sobbing and didn't want to go in, the security ladies understood and took me instead into a smaller training room. I sat in a chair and Joanne, our wonderful canteen lady, brought a bowl of water and towels to help clean me up.

They all seemed startled and realised how badly I had been hit when I spat a tooth out into the bowl. I remember thinking how glad I was that he missed my nose! Surely a victim shouldn't have to have such feelings as,

"Well at least it wasn't my nose!"

I settled down, stopped sobbing, stopped shaking, and a police officer came in to take my statement. He was genuinely nice, he had taken other witness statements, looked at me and said,

"In your own words, can you tell me what happened?"

I opened my mouth to start speaking and no words would come, all I could hear were my own sobs as I started to shake again.

The police officer decided I should just give my statement at a later date, and one of the security ladies took me to the hospital for x-rays, and obviously the dentist. The driver was sacked by his company, and when it got to court, he was given a suspended sentence. I was advised to apply to the government for compensation. Which I did and was awarded £325. Which I have spent ten times over on false/partial teeth and dental work in the years since.

Of course, when I got back to work, there were plenty of people who would have been tough or think they wouldn't have been hit. I'm afraid if someone hits you when you're not looking, there's not much you can do about it, and that person is a complete coward. The only person who said anything that I genuinely believed he could back up was Brian the bread man, who said to me,

"If I'd been there Ger, he wouldn't have walked out of here!"

With one tooth knocked clean out, there was one left. However, the gum above had been severely damaged, and it remained loose. The dentist asked me to wait a week for the swelling to go down before he assessed the viability of the remaining tooth.

I went back the next week. The dentist asked me to lay back in the chair and relax. Explaining he was just going to feel for the root. He had his dental pliers in his hand, I lay back, closed my eyes and relaxed with my mouth wide open.

I felt his pliers around the tooth, then he just pulled one quick motion and it was out. I yelled out loud!

Okay I screamed!

He explained there was nothing left holding it and that was the quickest kindest thing he could do.

I hope he was able to explain that to the patients outside in his waiting room, as my blood curdling screams echoed through his corridors.

11. CELEBRATING

Christmas and New Year in retail are always remarkably busy, and hard work. Staff work like crazy, it's only fair in the background they play hard and crazy too. In the huge department store on New Year's Eve, even though it was a Saturday, they were closing the store at 2 p.m. To compensate for letting everyone leave at 2 p.m. we all had to be there at 6 a.m.

I had no idea how I was going to be out of bed and ready for work at 5:45 a.m. Except, yeah, you guessed it, I did the only sensible thing and stayed up all night so I wouldn't sleep in.

What an idiot. Not only had this plan been a massive failure previously, but it wasn't going to work this time either.

There I was 5:45 a.m. marching off to work, we lived close, it was only a 210 second walk door to door. The fresh air kept me awake, and so did standing up at work keeping busy.

To celebrate New Year's Eve, each little department was bringing something for everyone else to enjoy. For example, I brought in a portable stereo record player, some of the lads and lasses in our department brought in some records we would sing along to, with the occasional dance move thrown in for laughs. In typical fashion the butcher's department had been a little more adventurous and one of the blokes had brought in a keg of beer, courtesy of his brother who just happened to work at a local brewery.

The beer wasn't opened or touched until the store was emptied and the departments were cleaned down, around about noon time. Then after a few drinks, we played a game where you had to lie on the floor beneath the tap of the keg while someone switched it on and see who could drink the most from the free-flowing tap on the keg three feet above.

Apart from nearly drowning, with beer splashing all over your hair and clothes, you were guaranteed to smell like a drunken pirate sleeping in the park, apologies to any drunken pirates, but you know what I mean.

As it came time to leave, everyone was agreeing to meet up later and have a great time for New Year's Eve, at one of the pubs. I thought great, I'll go home and have a nap for an hour or two, wake up and go out again later with my mates.

I got home sat on the edge of my bed and began to undo the some of the laces on my Doc Martins, these are the times you wonder why you wore footwear with thirteen lace holes. That's all I remember until 11 p.m. The pubs and bars all served last drinks in those days at 10:30 p.m.

I woke up, ran downstairs and asked my mother why on earth she hadn't woken me up. Turns out, not only had she tried to wake me up, but she had also allowed a procession of my friends to line up outside my bedroom and take turns going into my room, trying to wake me up by slapping and shaking me, exactly like a scene from a comedy movie, where they took turns in trying to shake me awake, then letting me drop back to my pillow.

Ever since that evening, I've never believed anyone who said they were too drunk to remember, but I will believe anyone who says they were too tired to remember.

Once again staying up all night instead of going to bed early proved a disaster. All I can say is that it's a good job teenagers know best, and exactly as my dad always said, New Year's Eve at a pub is overcrowded and overrated, although I wouldn't find that out this particular year.

Photo Booths were our source of selfies on those days. Losing my teeth was a horrible experience but we still used it to have laughs. Below me n Jim showing off my new falsies.

12. WILLIE

I moved on from the superstore and landed a job as a trainee shoe shop manager. My new boss, we'll call him Willie, was about six feet four inches tall, weighed around 120 kg (around 264 lbs) and had a strange sense of humour.

Either that, or he was just strange.

In December 1979, we were having a staff night out for Christmas. He and I weren't from the town, so to go home and get changed then return for a night out just wasn't practical, to make things easy, we would get changed from our suits to casual wear after the store closed in the staff room.

Then we would wait for our partners to arrive and together we would then head out to meet the rest of the staff at the chosen restaurant.

The shop closed, the staff went home to get changed and meet us at the restaurant. He and I were alone together and had to go into the "staff room" to change out of our suits into more casual wear.

While we were getting changed, he decided to tell me a joke where the punchline involved a man in a public lavatory talking to another man while peeing. The joke ends with one man turning towards the other man with his penis in his hand and peeing on the other man's shoes. Sadly, or thankfully, I can't remember the joke. Except, I have seen a Michael Caine interview on the chat show, "Parkinson" stating that John Wayne gave him some advice as a young actor, telling him never to wear suede shoes for that exact reason, as when people recognize you in the toilets they tend to forget what they're doing and turn towards you in surprise at being in the toilets with someone famous.

My boss Willy, went to such great lengths to illustrate the joke, that when it came time to tell the punchline, he made sure he was stripped down wearing only his Y-fronts and able to get his penis out while he turned towards me, gesturing the peeing on the imaginary bloke next to him in a public toilet, thankfully I wasn't stood too close.

I have always regarded myself as having a great sense of humour, and of being fairly broadminded, but I have to admit, this was a new one, a six foot four, biggish framed, well let's say fat bloke, who was my manager, was now stood in front of me, wearing only his Y-fronts, wagging his todger around, I think hoping I'd be impressed or something even worse, and framing it with a joke.

I don't know how many times he must have practiced this particular joke, either stood in front of a mirror, or mentally preparing for the time he gets a young trainee alone in the staffroom one time near Christmas, (thankfully no mistletoe) but as I'd always been told, if it's not something you can do in front of your family and friends then it probably isn't suitable for the workplace, and even then, some of things which are suitable for your family and friends shouldn't be in the workplace, just don't do these things.

I was stunned as to how I should respond. Thoughts ran through my head all at the same time.

"I mean, was it funny? No!"

"Was it appropriate? No!"

"Was he too big for me to try and be aggressive? Yes!"

"Was he my boss? Yes!"

"Had I done anything to attract this? No!"

With all these thoughts and more racing through my brain, I simply blurted out,

"Oh! Ha-ha, yeah good one!"

Then I immediately thought about all the people I couldn't possibly share the joke or the telling of the joke with, which turned out to be anyone and everyone.

I should have been glad that the joke didn't involve two blokes kissing, or a bloke plunging a knife into another bloke's chest.

Without too much further thought I hastened to finish getting ready, I don't think I've ever got dressed quicker than that in my whole life.

In fairness, I had worked there three months so he may have thought it was about time I saw his todger.

I didn't report him to HR, but I did mention it to Mrs Pat, the shop supervisor. She was worse than HR and made sure that I was never left alone with Willie again. Then coincidentally within a matter of weeks, I was lucky enough to be transferred to another location. Thankfully never to see Willie again.

13. TRAVELING LIGHT

The shoe company decided to open a small unit in the back of a clothing store in a small border town called Hawick. Any American readers should note it's not pronounced

"Hay-wick,"

it's pronounced

"Hoy-ck."

I was volunteered to go and help by the district manager. And although he was a short man, standing only around five foot five inches tall, he was a real disciplinarian. I was told Alan would pick me up in his car.

"Alan has a car?" I asked, shocked that Alan, who was in the same position as me, could afford a car, while I was struggling to pay for bus fare, cigarettes and beer.

"Yes," replied the area manager, "he passed his driving test a few months ago and volunteered to pick you up at the Newcastle bus station!"

"Oh! Great, erm thank you! Where is Hawick?" I had never heard of the town before, and thought I knew most places in the north.

"Don't worry, Alan knows the way and will get you there and bring you back." Was the not so detailed response from my boss. Well I wasn't going to buy a map, and back in the shop, Sid just said that it was somewhere on the Scottish border.

On the morning in question, I arrived at the bus station in plenty of time to wait for Alan to come along and pick me up. He couldn't drive into the bus station, which in Newcastle-

Upon-Tyne, was huge, so I figured sensibly enough to wait on the road running beside the bus station, which would be a dead end to the back of the shop where I was normally working.

Alan pulled up, now I could see why he had a car and I didn't. They were selling more expensive vacuum cleaners in the shops than this car would have cost.

It was an Austin Maxi; I was hoping he was going to tell me that he had borrowed it from his grandad. This car was truly awful and designed for people who didn't like his or her car to be sporty, comfortable or of practical use in any way. Mustard in colour, not an estate car, but looking like half an estate, nothing like a hot hatch, more like a hot potato.

We set off and to compensate for the car's shortcomings, Alan felt he had to try and show off, driving with his right foot rooted to the floor. This was proving quite scary, when we hit an open piece of road, and I noticed we were up to ninety mph.

This was truly a Star Trek moment where Scotty screams to Kirk at warp factor ten, something along the lines of,

"She cannae tek it Captain!"

There might not be many things quite as scary as being a passenger, whilst the driver was a young man, barely passed his driving test, smoking a cigarette, and trying to wind his window up and down (with a hand winder not electric) while going ninety miles an hour.

"Erm, Alan, I don't have a change of underwear, and I don't want to die in an Austin Maxi, while trying to overtake every single car we come upon!" I exclaimed!

"Why wots wrang with yer man?" Alan acted all surprised.

"Well it's single lane traffic, it's dangerous to try and overtake stuff, and I've never been on this road before and it might be nice to enjoy the view." I said in my "most trying to be reasonable voice."

The threat to our life, wasn't impressing him, but I think he thought that enjoying the view sounded like a good idea, plus if he drove at the speed limits, he could relax and chat a bit more, apparently, the shop we were going to was called a "concession shop," in the back of a large Scottish retail clothing, haberdashery and housewares outlet called "MacKay's."

Now we were driving at normal speeds and able to chat, he felt this was a great opportunity to brag that he was going to be the manager of this new small in store unit we were going to set up.

We drove straight to the department store, in the middle of Hawick, in which we occupied approximately five hundred square feet in the rear, with a lockable door to a stockroom.

Our illustrious vertically challenged leader and district manager was already there along with Maxine, who was a nice young lady from the merchandising and display team and her boss Ian. We all got stuck into the task in hand, and we were making great progress. At 6 O'clock, they decided to call it a day, and we would resume filling the display shelves tomorrow.

At this point I was expecting a repeat of Alan's wonderful driving for two hours to take us back to Newcastle upon Tyne.

Nope, surprise, we're all staying overnight, apparently, I was the only one who hadn't been told, we were staying at a local hotel. Not just an ordinary hotel, the district manager, had booked us into Mansfield House, a genuinely nice hotel. All I had on me was a half a packet of fags, a lighter, and a couple of quid. I couldn't believe it. There was no protesting, not to Napoleon, our area manager. Everybody went to their rooms to get changed before dinner. I went to my room to look at myself in the mirror and wonder what on earth I was going to do.

To put this in context, not only had I never set foot in a hotel before, but this was also a posh hotel. The kind you see in the movies, where they make you put a tie on to be able to tell you apart from the riff raff who apparently can't afford ties.

I didn't change for dinner, though I did "freshen" up by washing my hands and splashing some water on my face. I can't remember dinner; I remember afterwards everyone went into the lounge to be amazed by the newest feature the hotel had.

The door opened into the lounge, a sprawling room with grandiose furnishings, and there in the middle of the room, a large modern television which looked out of place with the other furniture and sitting on the floor in front of the television, their latest feature, the video recorder (VCR).

A big black box looking piece of equipment with huge sticking out keys. This was so new, that television stands to incorporate a VCR hadn't yet been invented.

"So how does this work then?" The district manager asked nobody in particular.

Ian the display manager, seemed to know all about these devices, while the rest of us stood and looked puzzled he replied,

"You plug your arial into the back of that, then feed it through to the television. Then if there's a television programme you want to record, you put a blank tape cassette in the machine and record the show."

"Huh?" Me and Alan both quizzically said in unison, "Why would you want to do that?"

Clearly, neither of us were up to date with anything going on in the world of television.

"Well," Ian continued, "You can watch one channel while recording a different channel to watch later or record a favourite movie to watch whenever you want, or even better, you can set it to record something while you're not home!"

Wow! How little did we realise that this black box VCR would revolutionise the way everyone enjoyed home entertainment.

"Whey that'll be no good at home!" Alan said.

"Yeah!" I agreed, "Nobody's going to want to watch television programmes over and over again."

This was spring 1980, clearly forecasting futures was not in my nor Alan's horizon.

After dinner, it was a relatively early night, but that was just the beginning of my problems.

I didn't have clean underwear; in fact I didn't have any clean clothes. The thought of having to wear the same socks the next day was terrifying to me, Miami Vice hadn't been made yet, so the bare foot in shoes, wearing no socks thing wasn't done. No toothbrush, no dental bath for my partial, no shaving foam or razor blades, no shampoo or soap. I'd left all of those things behind in my digs at Newcastle. Oh yes of course, hotels carry some of those things, but I didn't know.

The next morning, I did the best I could, no matter how hard I tried, my hair wouldn't lay down flat. The display girl Maxine was in the room next door, she knocked on my door to get me for breakfast.

I opened my door a little so I could talk to her, and close to tears I blurted out,

"I can't go, and I need to find a way to sneak out of the hotel without being seen!"

Maxine thought I was joking, laughed and said, "Oh of course, we can tie some sheets together and you can just drop out of the window, hug the side of the building then dash across the patio lawn and wait by the cars!"

"No, really!" I said, "I didn't know we were spending the night, I thought Alan was taking me back to Newcastle last night and so I didn't bring any toiletries, and everything is a mess, and I only have the one shirt!"

"Oh is that all! Ha-ha!" Maxine said, laughing louder, "Hang on I'll be back in a minute, don't go sneaking out commando style just yet!"

With that, I watched Maxine disappear down the corridor. Oh no! I shouldn't have said anything, now for sure she was going to tell the district manager, and I would be a complete idiot, imagine employing someone who didn't bring an overnight bag, never mind that the chief idiot didn't tell the junior idiot that he would be staying overnight. Either way, looking like a bunch of idiots in a country hotel wasn't a good look for anybody.

After what seemed like an eternity, okay, four and a half minutes, there was another knock on my door. Maxine was back, I opened the door and she waltzed in laughing,

"Here ya go!" She said as she handed me a toothbrush, toothpaste, shampoo, soap, a comb and a fresh pair of socks.

"Huh! Wow, thank you! I'll, I'll pay you for these when I get back!" I said. (Remember a life before cash machines).

Maxine laughed again and said, "No silly! These aren't off me. Ha-ha! They're from the front desk, and I've added them to the bill for the company at the hotel, so not a problem. Even our tight district manager isn't going to argue about toiletries on the bill."

"So the desk has these things if I'm stuck?" I asked.

"Yes!" Maxine couldn't help her laughing, "Omg, ha-ha and if you now go in the bathroom, get showered and dried, with the towels they let you use, I'll get the iron and quickly run over your shirt to freshen that up."

"You have an iron too?"

"No silly, every room, even yours, has an iron now go and get cleaned up!"

Maxine may have only been two years older than me but in terms of sophistication, maturity and experience, she was hundreds of years ahead of me.

They say chivalry is dead, well I don't think so, Maxine was my knight in shining armour that morning, and in one embarrassing trip I had learned enough to confidently be able to go anywhere, anytime and be comfortable, or had I?

14. SKINNY DIP

After training was completed in Newcastle-Upon-Tyne, it was time to say goodbye to the staff and store manager Sid and began my journey on the managerial merry go round.

Alan had been given the job of managing the new concession store in Hawick, the district manager decided to move me to the other Scottish border town Mackay's concession store in Berwick-Upon-Tweed. We had trained together and now we were both being given similar opportunities, although I must say, Berwick-Upon-Tweed is much busier than Hawick.

At Berwick I would have to live in accommodations in a small hotel called "The Ness Gate Hotel," close to the town centre.

The hotel might not have been very big, but it certainly had an impressive bar. The owner ran the bar himself, and he suggested that once I'd put my bags in my room and had something to eat in the dining room, I should go down to the bar, as there were a few others I might like to meet also staying on long term room rentals.

The fact that there were some other retail workers living there long term meant that at least my evenings would potentially not be filled by me sitting in my room staring at the walls. Even if they were all a little older than I was and had a slightly different sense of humour.

After I'd eaten I walked into the bar and the hotel owner introduced us to one another.

"Hey lads," said the owner, and now the barman, "this is Ben, he'll be staying the summer while he works in town, and I've put him in the other attic room next to you."

"Aye cheers!" Said Dave in his broad Scottish accent, then he looked me up and down and asked, "Sew where are ye working Ben?"

"I'm working in Mackay's managing the shoe dept for Curtess Shoes." I said, while proudly smiling at all three of them

Colin who worked with and shared a room with Dave, immediately latched on to the last words I spoke, and as he laughed at his own humour he said,

"Och aye, Curtess like the famous film actor Tony Curtis, that's it then, we'll carl yer Tony frae noo on!"

"Erm but that's not my name ha-ha!" Was my meekly attempted rebuff.

"Och aye reetio Tony!" Colin and Dave said in unison.

The third bloke, had been quiet, he was tall and thin, he looked older than all of us, and he leaned forward held out his hand to shake and as he spoke it was evident he was very English said,

"Pleased to meet you Tony. I'm Alan, the manager of MacKay's!"

"Oh ha-ha! That's great, at least I can walk into the store with you tomorrow morning."

"Sure," Alan said, "Now lad's let's buy Tony a drink."

"Aye cheers," replied Dave, "I'll have a pint o heavy!"

"Aye, me too! But just the one more for the neet, am on earlies the mornin!"said Colin.

"D'yer want us ter chap yer up in the morning, afore breakfast?" Asked Dave.

"Uh I dunno, what does that mean?" I cautiously replied.

"Och aye, ha-ha! He's a Sassenach alreet!" Laughed Colin.

They were all laughing, and Alan said to me, "They're giving you a hard time, ha-ha, it means to knock on your door to wake you up in the morning."

"Yes, yes, that would be great," I replied laughing, "though I think I'm gonna need a translator hanging out with you lot!"

"Och-aye, yer will," laughed Colin and Dave out loud, "You're gonna learn many barry and coosty words hanging out with us and the locals ha-ha!"

After a frustrating week or two where I learned that the locals closely protect their language and uses from outsiders, or they just liked laughing at my not knowing, eventually I was informed that "Barry and Coosty" were local words used to describe something as good, or exceptionally good.

Despite my protests, every time we would go out for a night to a new pub and meet new people, they would introduce me as Tony, in their heavy brogue Scottish accent, so it sounded even funnier when I would say in my squeaky north east England accent,

"No, that's not my real name!"

Then they would reply in unison, "Och Aye Tony, if you say so Tony!"

Back in those days, the bars would close between 10:30 p.m. and 11p.m. That time of night in northeast England in summer would never really get pitch black dark and when the moon was up, visibility was almost just like a shadowy day, especially if you'd had a drink or two.

On such a night, we all decided to walk the long way back to the hotel we lived in, going parallel to the street the hotel was on, across the side of the golf course down via the small harbour, adding around an extra ten minutes, and on a beautiful bright summer night, a good idea to walk some of the beer off.

I always remember Berwick harbour from those times as very calm, and it certainly was on this bright night.

Colin said, "Hey! Let's jump in the watta fer a laugh, we can have a daft game of tag."

Everyone was laughing,

"Och-aye sure!" Dave said.

I thought they were being sarcastic and I certainly never took the suggestion seriously, not until Colin was stripped naked and climbing down the metal harbour ladder into the water.

There he was completely naked, telling us how it wasn't very deep, and we would be able to run around. We were all laughing, as he said

"Haway mon! Get yersells in and we'll have a game of tig! (Tag)"

I was very reluctant, I could give you a list of about 500 reasons not to go in the sea at night, mine were mainly to do with not being a strong swimmer, and not having a body that you would want to show off, not even in the dark. In fact, in moonlight I would look like a slither of light shimmering off the water.

The other two started to undress,

"Ha-ha, okay then, I'll get in!" I said thinking I should join in.

Good old peer pressure. Taking off my clothes and stacking them beside the harbour steps, I climbed down the steel ladder, got into the water, it wasn't deep, only waist high, so you could move quite easily. I had left my tennis shoes on to manoeuvre with my feet on the ground without cutting my feet on any sharp stones, plus it would be easier to get around and I began to chase after Colin.

I don't think we had any rules, I'd figured they immediately put the onus on me to tag the others coz I was the youngest.

Colin was moving further out, I was ever mindful that we shouldn't get too far away from the wall and shouted,

"Hey, Colin, you can't go too far from the wall, it might get too deep!"

He appeared to listen to me as he cut back towards the harbour wall. I turned to try and reduce his advantage by chasing him back to the wall.

I could see Dave and Alan were still on the harbourside laughing. They still had all their clothes on, when just a moment ago, I was sure they were following me down the steps. I was about thirty feet from the wall, Colin was almost back to the wall, in fact, Colin was almost back to the steps.

He reached the steps and scurried up them out of the water like a harbour rat, I shouted straight away,

"Hey he's cheating! That's not fair!"

The response from all three of them immediately changed my thoughts on the situation I was now in. All three of them were crippled doubled up with laughter.

There I was slicing through the water as fast as I could, trying desperately to close that thirty-foot gap. Even as thin and whispery as I was, it still felt like I was knee deep in a tub of treacle.

I could see Colin pulling his clothes back on. Then he turns around and shouts,

"Och aye cheers Tony! See you later!"

"Hey, wait for me yer bastads!" I shouted as I was nearing the steps.

To make matters worse, I could see as the three of them ran off up the hill, Colin had picked up all of my clothes and was laughing so hard he was struggling to run.

I made it out of the water, just in time to see them disappear up the lane and head back across the golf course towards the road that would lead back down to the hotel.

The easy way was to walk along the harbour, under the bridge and back along the side street to the hotel, but I was naked except for my white tennis shoes, they had my clothes, and I couldn't be sure there wouldn't be normal nice people out for a moonlit walk.

The only thing for it was to try and catch up to them and get my clothes back before they got to any areas where there were houses.

Great, now I have to run naked, not that it made much difference, I wasn't a good runner with my clothes on so I wasn't any better naked, at least I had my tennis shoes on. I ran after them up onto the field, I could hear them laughing but couldn't quite see them, at least I was on their trail.

I followed the sound of laughter and halfway across there was one of my socks, ha-ha very funny, then a few feet further, the other sock. About thirty feet further just before the roadway were my Y-fronts, my bright tighty whities highly visible in the bright moonlight.

I ran out of golf course grass and there were no more clothes. I couldn't hear them laughing anymore. They must've headed back onto the street and back to the hotel.

I would have to sneak back through the streets wearing only Y-fronts, socks and tennis shoes. I got to the road the hotel was on, a quick glance up and down told me the street was deserted, and truthfully I was more worried about the police than the public.

I mean imagine the headline in the local Gazette,

"Midnight Madness. Shoe Shop Manager aka Tony Curtess, Streaks through the Streets!"

Being skinny had its advantages, hopefully anyone glancing in my direction would just think his or her imagination was playing up, people looking out of their windows confused and asking each other,

"Was that a streaker?"

"Did I just see a nearly naked man running around Berwick in his Y-fronts?"

"No, don't be silly dear, it was just the moonlight playing tricks with your eyesight!"

Mercifully, they had left the front door of the hotel unlocked, I walked in through the big double doors, and there halfway up the stairs were the rest of my clothes.

"Bastads!" Was all I could think, but still giggling at how they had really got me good.

The hotel owner popped his head out of the bar and laughingly said,

"The lads are wanting to know if you fancy a nightcap before you go up to bed? Colin said you might want a Dry Vermouth. Then again Colin's jokes were never that funny."

The hotel owner knew us all very well and enjoyed the laugh, his more respectable guests had already retired for the evening, meanwhile we all had a laugh and joke in the hotel bar, about how gullible I was, and about how clever they were able to plan and execute it before we left the last bar.

That was a great summer in 1980, as they might say in Berwick, "We had a barry or coosty time!" And while we never did go skinny dipping again, we did play tag on the main bridge over the River Tweed while it was scaffolded for renovations.

15. MY SHOP

Alan got promoted from the Hawick concession to run the small shop in Darlington, at the same time I was promoted to manage my first shop, with its own front door under lock and key, to the Curtess shoe shop on Newport Rd, Middlesbrough. Great place, six of us aged under twenty, and two part time ladies in their thirties, and as such we called them, "the auld ladies!"

I took charge of the shop in September, after a fun and busy summer running the Berwick concession, having my own shop was a great feeling.

Mrs Pat from my Hartlepool days was in charge until I was taking over permanently, she would show me around and introduce me to the staff. The main fulltime employee was Betty, called that because she was the girl with Betty Davis eyes. Together they showed me around the building. Walking through the stockrooms upstairs, there was a padlocked door to an attic room.

"What's up there?" I asked.

"Dunno." Said Pat, "no one ever goes up there, that I know of."

"You've never been up there?" I asked quizzically.

"No I was never bothered, and Betty here is new, so she's never been up there either."

"Wow, I dunno how you can't go exploring." I said laughing, "let's go get the key then."

I ran back down the stairs, got back up, catching my breath and asked,

"Right, are we going up?"

"I'm not bothered." Pat said.

"I'll go." Said Betty in her soft voice.

I took the padlock off, eased the door open to reveal a small spiral stairway. Despite my inherent lack of bravery, I thought it suitable that I should go first, I mean, I could have sent Betty up first, but then I would be exactly like my first bosses in deciding the expendability of the people around me ha-ha!

I walked up the hidden winding staircase, above my head was the hatch to the attic, I pulled the bolt back and pushed the hatch lid upwards and climbed up. Unsurprisingly, there were no fanfares or booby traps. A big empty loft room with two windows in the side of the roof.

Betty came up behind me and stepped into the light. The attic was so clean and bright, especially after being in the dark and dreary stock rooms.

The room was more like an unfurnished secret bedroom with a window in the roof facing the street, too inaccessible to be useful for storing anything for the shop, but you could imagine hiding there and just watching the world go by outside. Neither Betty nor I said a word, but we both knew, in that moment and time if someone had closed the attic hatch, then we would still be there now. Forever a summer afternoon, the light coming through the window, our very own secret place.

Back down we went, locked the room up again, and went back down the main stairs and through to the rear of the building which used to be a house but now had an unsafe second story boarded up, even the staircase leading up to the sealed area was in unsafe condition, I never did get to exploring that part of the old shop, besides Pat said,

"As long as I've known that has been boarded up for years, and that floor has been closed due to safety concerns!"

That part of the building where the disused stairs came down was quite spooky, even haunted, or as some would say nowadays, "it had a lot of character," which means it had never been cleaned nor had a light shone inside for forty years.

I still have nightmares revolving around that building at the rear. In my nightmare I climb through a small hole in the back wall to go into the upstairs, suddenly it becomes a monstrous unsafe old building, bigger than Downton Abbey with cavernous stairways and hallways leading to rooms that I have to navigate to try and find the room where people are waiting for me with an exit back to the real world. I never find the way out, usually I end up being chased or falling backwards unable to move forwards or find my way through the labyrinth.

After a couple of days, Pat returned to Hartlepool and I was left in charge of my new young team. I had never felt the need to subscribe to the "tough boss" club, in the way the district manager would like, and at the first, and only small staff meeting, I simply said,

"You will all think I have a funny laugh, and a funny walk, and whilst those things are both true, I'd rather you laugh with me than at me, and while our district manager would like you to call me Mr. Teeley, I am fine with you calling me Mr. T." (Yes I know but this was before the "A" Team ha-ha).

We got on like a house on fire, because we were all of a similar age group there was a great rapport among us, I could tell in other shops with older managers that there was no way they had the same connection with their staff.

The first Christmas Eve, I told them we could close the shop early, company protocol was to open until 6 p.m. However, the street was quiet, and in retail it had become the normal thing to do, it was 2 p.m. We had done well, and I had some work to do upstairs to get the sale stock ready for the days after Christmas.

After about half an hour, there was a shout from Jimmy at the bottom of the stairs,

"Hey! Mr. T. There's a little bald man outside the front door, he says I have to let him in! I've told him we're closed but he said to go and get you immediately!"

Yup, my district manager was still the same, five-foot five-inch Napoleon, little bald fella, tough as nails with a zero-tolerance attitude. I nearly fell down the stairs running three or four steps at a time, trying to get to the front door. I'm sure anyone listening thought I had thrown the fridge and the microwave down the stairs.

With each leap I was trying to think up a good excuse why I would close the shop four hours early.

"I was sick!"

"The staff were sick!"

"We had a bomb scare, ha-ha!"

I burst through the door at the bottom of the stairs, turned the corner, only to see everyone laughing hysterically. No way was Napoleon visiting locations on Christmas Eve, he was at home with his feet up drinking sherry, while my staff laughed hysterically at catching me out.

Never mind being called "Mr. T". I was more the epitome of "Pity the Fool!" and certainly one of the biggest suckers around.

Being of a similar age and working forty hours a week together you do get close to people. Betty and I were the only two full time staff in the shop all week, with the others rotating in and out part time or as required. One afternoon, prior to closing, we were fun fighting, I've no idea how or why these things started. Betty was five feet four inches tall (in her heels) I was six feet (OK in my heels too). Betty would often try to scratch me with her nails. There was a flat wall behind the cash register, and on this occasion, I had managed to grab both of her hands, put them above her head and pressed her flat to the wall.

Our mouths and noses were only an inch apart, we were both breathing heavy, yet almost breathless. I remember looking into her eyes, deep into her very heart and soul.

At this point in the movies we would kiss, Whitney Houston would be singing, "And I will always love you," the audience wipe away their tears and everyone lives happily ever after.

We didn't.

One of those life moments you can reflect upon and ask the question, "What if?"

A moment that would be in my Armageddon flashback, where I'm Bruce Willis and I see every life event as I press the button, and that moment is in there, Betty looking back at me, while Kim Carnes is singing in the background, "She's got Betty Davis eyes!"

I can never explain why or how we never became an item, that's not arrogance, just chemistry. We did go on to become close, even having more fun fights, I can't remember how or why they started, but they were always funny.

I still hear Betty answer the shop phone then shout up the stairs for me,

"Teeee!" in her loudest voice.

Usually, it was Napoleon the district manager who was on the phone, and as I picked up the receiver, he would always say to me in a rather droll Orson Welles kind of voice,

"Do they have to shout for you like that?"

Truth is, I liked it, and as I was his only shop out of twenty-four in North England not producing negative sales results, he tended to cut me a lot of slack. If you're wondering just how good that made me look, google the 1979 UK recession.

16. **WHAT GOES AROUND**

As manager of my first small shop in Middlesbrough I first met Gail, she was a Saturday girl. Ha-ha don't worry, that name didn't mean anything bad, just a name used at the time for students employed part time to work a few hours after school and of course on Saturdays.

Nowadays I'm sure the term would be revised to accommodate all days of the week and all sexual orientations. The main thing was they were low cost and keen to work to earn money while still at school.

Gail was the youngest when I took over the shop, but every bit as reliable as anyone else working there. To help out over the busy Christmas periods I decided to employ the younger brothers of Betty Davis eyes and Carla. These two young men were a little younger than Gail, and certainly contributed to the balance of the team. Gail enjoyed moving up in the pecking order. Especially when it came to doing stock duties in the dark and damp cold basement.

For almost two years I worked with Gail, she was always very guarded and at her young age I could tell she expected me to behave much more managerially and seriously.

She would definitely have preferred to call me Mr. Teeley, and certainly was always the one the others would turn to if they wanted me to believe something was true.

I would even say Carla and I would use Gail as a barometer for the level of seriousness when we were laughing at something silly.

Carla went to see the comedy duo "Cannon and Ball" and for the next two months she would walk around saying one of their catchphrases,

"Have you got the time on yer cock?"

Then she would laugh for five minutes after each time she said it, I would laugh a little but Gail never really figured that it was that funny and would never fake a false laugh when something just wasn't funny, and truthfully it just wasn't really that funny.

You could tell Gail was destined to go on and have a successful career and be the person in charge.

In a strange twist of fate nineteen years later I pulled into the car park of the business where I had a scheduled interview. As I began walking towards the building there was Gail walking in. I smiled and you could see the recognition coming flooding back to her face. Her smile lit up as she exclaimed,

"Mr. Casanova"

"Oh ha-ha! Almost!" I replied, "I'm Mr. Teeley, Mr. Casanova was the manager who hired you before I took over."

Gail burst out laughing and said, "Oh of course! Now I remember!"

We exchanged a quick overview of how the last nineteen years had gone, and she asked me what I was doing there? I explained I was going for an interview. Turns out Gail was in a senior position in the organisation and very well thought of.

Now I can't say for a fact that Gail got me the job, but Gail got me the job. I walked in with her practically arm in arm and laughing, remembering Carla and Betty Davis Eyes et al. Gail did me the courtesy of introducing me to the H.R. and training people personally. To make this position even more significant it set me on the path to be with the people who would have an even bigger impact on my life and see me moving to America.

So "Thank you!" Gail.

I would not be sitting where I am today if not for your kindness in helping me get the position. As I look back, who knows where I would have ended up!

At the time of getting the position, I was a salesperson, not making a lot of money, contemplating moving to London to be a bus driver. This job meant I could stay in the North, regroup from a separation and relaunch myself again.

You should always be nice to the people you meet. You truly never know when they will enter your life again, or the impact he or she may have on your future.

17. **STANDING AROUND**

Stockton on Tees was my next stop. Mr. Casanova was the manager I was replacing, yes, the same Mr. Casanova who had hired Gail in the previous store. He was a tall thin angry looking young man, with a military haircut. He eventually went on to become a police officer.

Casanova had no problem upsetting his customers. Often, they would demand the address or phone number to his head office so they could make a complaint. Casanova would always give them my information. Only one sticks in my mind, a lovely lady wrote a letter complaining about the slippers she had purchased and the treatment she had received when complaining. I felt so bad for her and asked her if she could make it to my location at Middlesbrough. She came and I exchanged the slippers for her and told her he would be chastised. Not sure how credible she thought I was though, standing there looking like an undernourished Oliver Twist in a suit pretending to be his boss.

Casanova had trained the "casual Saturday staff" at Stockton well. Okay I'm being sarcastic, but they were excellent at being very "casual." The gang of four teenagers would come in on a Saturday morning, then proceed to spend most of the day leaning against mirrors chewing gum, waiting to be annoyed by customers asking for help.

The only thing they could have possibly done worse was pop open a can of beer. When I took over, there was no way I was going to have the same rapport as I'd experienced in my last shop.

In addition to the apathy of the Saturday staff, the full-time employee Laura, was disengaged because just before I took over, she had her hours cut down from forty to thirty-two due to the thirty percent decline in sales while Mr. Casanova was in charge.

This decline didn't look out of place with all of the other shops, (mine was the only one without a decline), and Mr. Casanova always kept his shop clean and tidy, so any visiting district manager would always think things are being "done correctly!" Ready for the upturn.

The first thing to do was to get Laura's buy-in, she wasn't very happy, and as she was the supervisor, if I could somehow get her firing on all cylinders she would support me in my efforts to get the rest of them going.

My first week there, I hardly spoke. I know there are those of you who know me shaking your head in disbelief that I could be so quiet, ha-ha! But even I know that sometimes watching is the best thing to understand what's going on.

Everything was almost done correctly, except the sales floor. I asked Laura and Doreen (the part-time lady),

"Why are you always out the back of the shop?"

"Mr. Casanova always told us to take care of the back and he would take care of the front!" They both volunteered.

"Oh, ha-ha! Well that certainly explains a lot," I said while laughing, "I mean how many customers must have been lining up outside the shop to be served by a sneering six-foot three skinhead ha-ha!" It was clear to me that this shop just wasn't a happy shop to enter, certainly nobody was smiling.

Laura and Doreen, didn't get it, "Well he served the customers and filled the gaps, until the Saturday staff came in!" Said Laura, thinking it was a great plan.

"Okay," I said, "I understand that stock has to be put away, and that things need looking after, but suppose we put the front first and take care of the back once the front is done?"

"I suppose so!" They both agreed.

"Laura," I said directly, "What would make you happiest about working here?"

"Well," she said, "I would like my forty hours back, I'm missing the money!"

"Okay," I said, "I can't change your contract back, but suppose I promise you at least eight hours a week overtime? Would you be happy then?"

"That would be great!" She said, "I'd gladly be onboard with that!"

"And you Doreen," I continued, "What would you like to see done to make you feel better at work?"

Now Doreen was slightly nervous, and nobody had ever asked for her input before, but I think she sensed that I would do what I could to help as long as they supported any changed I wanted to make, and she said rather boldly for her,

"Well, I think that we do all the work and the Saturday staff just come in and hang around!"

"Agreed," I said, "So if I fix the Saturday staff and get them working, then you'll also be onboard the good ship T?"

"Yes." Doreen, nodded in agreement.

"Right, well from now on," I said, beginning to outline my plans, "I want you two to focus on the sales floor, when at all possible. I'm sure customers would rather see you two than my ugly mug ha-ha. And when a customer walks in never ask, "can I help you?" simply smile at them, and walk past them as if you're busy, go to a stand pretty close to them, but never ask "can I help you?" Yes I've said that twice, but it's important, simply smile and if you do speak say, 'Good morning or afternoon' then go past them to dust a shoe or tidy something up, and I guarantee in ninety percent of cases the customer will ask you a question about something they have their eye on! As soon as that happens, they're interested in buying something"

I could see neither of them believed me, so I reiterated, "I'll be watching, and these are the only rules, always smile on the sales floor and never ask if you can help anyone! Do you think you can do that, if I take care of the Saturday staff work ethic and give you Laura eight hours overtime each week?"

Both of them gave me a fake sarcastic smile and nodded in agreement.

"Ha-ha!" I said, "Yes that's the stuff, big smiles, I know you don't believe me but I promise it will work. Now the Saturday staff, standing around chewing gum and polishing their nails, is that what they've normally been doing?"

"Yes." Said Doreen, "Normally one of them keeps busy and does stuff, but the other three tend to just stand around a lot until it's time to tidy up before we go home."

This was the early 1980's way before cell phone days, so they really did just stand leaning against the mirrors and look at their nails.

Saturday was a busy day, easily selling between 200 and 300 pairs of shoes. Once the shop had been open an hour, there were always gaps on the displays to fill, laces to straighten and racks tidy, especially on the outside promotional shelves. Basic retail maintenance, tidy, fill, and clean in between helping customers.

My second week, I asked the gang of four to come in fifteen minutes early for a meeting. I was polite, always smiling, basically repeating the same instructions I had given Doreen and Laura, with a few additions,

"When you see a gap on a shelf, fill it, if you don't have a customer to serve, go to the front street displays and tidy them up, and finally, if there's anyone who wants to lean on a mirror, polish their nails or chew gum on the sales floor they should leave now! If I see it happening again, I would be letting that person go!"

The next week, before we opened the shop, the tallest one, who had also assumed leadership of the gang of four said to me,

"According to my dad, you can't fire us for leaning on the mirrors and chewing gum!"

As always, I smiled, then replied,

"With all respect to your father, if you don't believe me then go ahead and lean on the mirrors and chew gum and I will fire you."

Nobody leaned on a mirror again, nobody chewed gum, sales increased by forty-two percent over the previous year, earning me a promotion to a huge shop later that year.

Bragging, of course I am. Willie, yes him with the bad penis joke, we talked about earlier in chapter twelve, had told me it took him eight and it would take me ten years before aspiring to such a position, I had done it in three, and I'm certain Mr.

Casanova went on to become an excellent policeman, and sadly I've no idea what happened to Alan out of Darlington.

18. ABANDON SHOP

I was promoted back to Hartlepool, the same location where I started my training with Willie and Mrs Pat. Hartlepool was a big shop, two shop units combined into one. Two entries from the sales floor to the stockroom, one to the men's side, the other to the ladies and children. Each side joined through a corridor at the rear and each with a fire exit. At the rear of the Women's stock section, was the break room. Through the fire exits, was a communal corridor, shared by other retailers, and on the other side of the corridor we had an overflow stockroom.

I tell you about the layout for good reason. A cold winter Thursday, I let all the staff leave at exactly 5:35 p.m. I remember it well. As soon as I turned the key to say goodnight, I realised I hadn't asked anyone if they had checked the stockrooms to make sure there were no security threats, more precisely no shoplifters hanging around the stockroom.

This was a problem with stockrooms having two entries from the sales floor, sometimes it was difficult to watch them from a security perspective. Occasionally you would find a "customer" in the stockroom, looking to see what they could filch quickly.

Not being noticeably big or brave, my heart sank, a part of me wanted to leave immediately, find someone off the street to come and help me with a quick search and lock up the back doors with me. Walking through the back, I could feel myself shaking, feeling sick. I wasn't worried about the ladies' side; all the staff had just walked through as they were leaving. I was worried about the men's side. The stock shelves were from floor to ceiling, so you couldn't see through them, and each side of the stockroom had five or six stock shelves, creating mini corridors down the aisle that anyone could hide behind.

My thoughts were,

"Do I leave?"

"Run?"

"Abandon ship?"

"Sound the evacuation!"

In my mind, I could already hear that noise a submarine makes in the movies during an emergency dive! I was listening as keenly as possible for any sound that might betray a thief.

I had encountered people in the stockrooms before, luckily, I always had loads of employees around me. We employed seventeen people, so the intruder always retreated, apologising, feigning that they were lost. In each of these instances, the intruders were always big and menacing.

Once there were two of them, the little one pointed to the big one behind him and said to me,

"He doesn't want to go back to prison, so do as we say, and you will be alright!"

I managed not to cry, kept my composure and replied,

"That's ok, if you leave now, I won't scream, nobody will report you and there won't be any going back to prison!"

Amazingly this worked, no threats, no tears, just facts and they left.

A friend managing a frozen food store around the corner wasn't so lucky, the one time he caught a shoplifter he called the police. The trouble was that exactly a week later, six of the shoplifters "friends" came into his shop and locked him in a big chest freezer. I still remember his employees coming running to me for help. Ha-ha can you imagine how much trouble you must be in if you're being assaulted by six people and I'm the one someone runs for to help you?

Luckily for the offenders, by the time I'd had a cigarette, a cup of tea, tied my shoelaces and strolled round to his store, they had fled the scene.

Back to my cold, dark, rainy Thursday in my oversized shoe shop, with thoughts running through my head.

"What would I do if I did catch someone?"

"What would they do to me?"

My eyes settled on a broom!

"Aha!" I proclaimed out loud.

Something to defend myself with, I gripped the bristle head of the broom tightly, pointing the handle out in front of me, like a knight of old armed with a lance. Trouble was, I still didn't feel very brave as I entered the stockroom with my lance pointing out in front of me.

Each shelf was about four feet wide, with an alleyway between about three foot six inches wide. I turned to look down the first aisle, broom handle in front of me pointing down the aisle ready to slay any dragons, or thieves, I wanted to shriek,

"En-Garde!" As I looked down the aisle.

Yeah, I know that is with a sword, but my brush could just have easily been my sword, and I needed to feel a sense of bravado.

My heart was beating faster than a drum rolling down a hill. The first aisle was all clear.

"Now what? What if the intruder had moved to the other aisle before I had even looked!"

"Do I walk slowly around, from aisle to aisle?"

Do I shout, "I know you're there?"

Any self-respecting criminal would just wait for me to walk around the corner, take the broom away from me and put it where the sun doesn't shine. As all good generals know, speed or surprise is the best option! I am standing in the stockroom facing down an aisle, a broom pointing down the aisle.

Behind me a wall, on my left the sales floor entry, to my right another thirty feet of stockroom and another four or five aisles to check. I calculated with one leap to my right, feet together, I could be suddenly staring down the next aisle.

That was the scene at 5:37 p.m. On a cold winter Thursday evening in the stockroom of my shoe shop. Skinny young man in a suit, leaping sideways between aisles, with a broom pointing out in front, shouting,

"Come out now and I'll let you go!" All the way to the rear of the stockroom.

Imagine doing the "Time Warp" without the music, and all the jumps to the right ha-ha!

I then went through the back doors, across the corridor, to the spare stock room, then back down the other side of the stock room, locking doors behind me. Nobody was there.

Later in life I would refuse to have anything to do with the opening and closing of the financial establishments I worked in. I reasoned that if I was going to stress about a shoe shop, then I would go berserk trying to secure a bank. Not sure how the rest of the bankers would react to the manager leaping around with a broom at closing time!

19. UNLIKELY LOCAL HERO

Christmas Eve 1980, I was at the bus station in Hartlepool. Late afternoon, between 5 p.m. and 6 p.m. In that part of England at that time of year, it is already dark and cold. Yes, this was the same bus station in which I had been applauded for eventually waking up alone on the top deck of a bus a few years earlier.

There was a path on my left-hand side which went past the bus station and continued towards the town centre. On the path walking towards the bus stops, from the town centre, around 200 feet in front of me, were two young women. You could tell they were both happily chit chatting and laughing, excited about Christmas.

Out of the corner of my eye walking towards the girls from the opposite direction, were three boisterous lads, with skinhead haircuts, drunk and loud. Two of them looked about six foot five inches tall, and not to be messed with, the other one was about my height, but with the added bonus of weighing about two or three times as much as I did and was also the shape and size of how you would imagine a scary troll emerging from under a bridge. None of them were really dressed for the weather, t-shirt and denim jackets. Anyone caring to glance in my direction would have politely described me as slight, more of a shadow passing under the lights, I was tallish, skinny, and wearing a suit, and definitely dressed for the weather, covered by my new snorkel parka coat.

The lads were clearly drunk and seemingly happy. The shortest one seemed to be the most boisterous and animated, trying to attract the attention of the girls. You might say rather unkindly that he was "aping around." I could hear him laughing and loudly suggesting that the girls should come with them to the next location for a drink.

As they got closer to the girls, the girls split apart to walk around the lads and let the lads carry on through the middle on the path. The girls were still laughing, clearly ignoring the suggestions that they should about turn and walk with the lads to the next bar.

The next part seemed to happen so quickly. I remember smiling, as the lads had tried to stop the girls to engage in a conversation with them, if that is possible for three drunken men to do. One girl had successfully navigated her way past the three lads, and was waiting for her friend, not standing around kind of waiting, just a split second where are you? Her friend, the other girl had almost made it past on the other side. The two tall lads were beside her and the stocky lad was behind her. The stocky lad had been asking her for a Christmas kiss, which she had declined, he turned around, still talking to her from behind, still asking her for a Christmas kiss, and began trying to kiss the back of her neck. At which point, she shrugged her shoulders and continued to move forward trying to take no real notice of him.

Suddenly, from behind her, the stocky lad placed both of his arms over her shoulders and grabbed both of her boobs. I looked at her friend who was still laughing, I was shocked, my first thought was,

"Oh! They must all know each other!"

The two taller lads were also laughing, my thoughts continued,

"That's not necessarily the way I would greet anyone I knew in the street, or even behind closed doors ha-ha, it seems a bit forward. However, with it being Christmas and everyone being jolly, having fun, and tipsy, they must be real good friends, they're all just having a laugh! Who am I to question how people have fun?"

The girl the troll was attacking was now looking straight at me, and in a split second her laughing had turned to shock, she now looked terrified, she began crying. Even from where I was standing I could see tears and shock, and through her sobbing, I could hear her say,

"Someone please help me!" I looked up and down the bus station, hoping there was a team of trained soldiers or a full team of Hartlepool rugby players behind me that she was really staring at.

Nope, she was definitely staring at me and asking for help, I double checked, glancing around, spinning on the spot, hoping that people had magically appeared behind me, like they do in the movies to save the day.

The bus station might as well have had tumbleweed blowing through it, there wasn't another single passenger, no buses had arrived yet, no drivers. I continued looking around up and down the street, there were no other people, there wasn't even a car driving past, no other soul in the world was there in that moment, just me, feeling cosy and warm all zipped up in my new snorkel parka coat, with my hood up.

I'm standing in what feels like a time capsule, I'm seeing everything in slow motion, but in reality, for this poor girl seconds had already passed. The two six foot five lads were telling him to leave her alone, to move on, he was laughing, telling them

"He was having fun!" They weren't physically trying to stop him.

I could see the pleading increase in the eyes of this girl, looking at me for help, tears rolling down her cheeks, and a sizable troll trying to molest her. He still hadn't moved his hands away from her boobs, her friend wasn't laughing anymore. Now, they both looked terrified. The two biggest lads while laughing kept saying,

"Haway man, leave the lass alern, let's go gerra nutha drink at the next bar!"

He kept ignoring them, laughing and thinking he was being funny, saying,

"Nah man! She's ganna gizza kiss fer Christmas!" As his groping of the young lady looked like it was becoming more aggressive.

If ever there was a time for someone to get out a mouth organ and start playing "The Good, The Bad and The Ugly" theme tune by Ennio Morricone, then this was surely it. I took my Parka hood down; I'd like to think the same way Clint threw his poncho over his shoulder but sadly not. I puffed my twenty-eight-inch chest out, and shouted in my biggest voice,

"Hoo man, it's Christmas Eve man! Leave her alone!"

I'd always been told I had a big mouth, and amazingly much to my surprise it worked. You could tell he had heard me by the way he just dropped all interest in the girl, plus the thudding noise his knuckles made hitting the floor as he let go of her when they dropped to his side.

Then, there was the swivelling noise his neck made as he turned towards where the sound had come from and his brain quickly asserted that this puny bloke in the parka couldn't possibly be talking to him. Yet not for another thirty years would a similar scene be portrayed on film as Orcs grunted and sniffed for the Hobbits outside the shire.

When I say it worked, it worked for the girl. She sensibly started to walk away from him with her friend. Now he was mad at me.

"Who the fuck d'yer think you're talkin to?" He shouted at me.

Oh shit! Now I was going to die at Hartlepool bus station on Christmas Eve, and not even make it to the 1980's, beaten to a pulp by three lads, well two lads and their pet troll. I could see the newspaper headlines,

"Shoe shop worker found well and truly scuffed!"

I looked across the street towards him, and repeated in my best big voice,

"It's Christmas man!"

I was hopeful he would break into a chorus of Jingle Bells or dance me a merry dance to the latest Christmas pop song while extolling the virtues of everyone getting along, because "It's Christmas!"

Needless to say, the Christmas spirit did not embrace him. Any one of these three lads, could, without breaking sweat do me some serious damage, especially since my fighting skills had extensively evolved around me hitting my opponent's fist with my face as many times as possible in the first three seconds of any fight I had been involved in, as told in "Ben's School Days!"

Suddenly there was an unexpected turn of events. The two biggest lads got hold of him and said,

"Come on! We don't need no trouble! Let's just go!"

Oh, my goodness! There is a God! Thank the Lord! It truly is Christmas!

He began getting angry with his taller friends,

"Nah!" He yelled! "He thinks he's a fuckin hardman!"

He certainly had that part wrong. I didn't feel like a tough man!

"Erm, no, no I don't!" I said, shaking my head, which was still sticking out of my oversized new parka, oh how I wished I could just put my hood back up and hide.

He continued to shout!

"Am ganner knack him!" (Which translates as beat me to a pulp).

He ignored the two lads he was with and began ambling towards me, looking like he had just learned to walk upright that week, continuing to grunt in my direction,

"Think yer tough huh?" He drunkenly sneered.

"Erm, no, no I don't thank you!" I said, trying to be polite.

"Well am ganna teach yer a lesson, ter not stick yer nose in my business!" He continued towards me.

I was even prepared to provide him with solid references which would testify to the fact that I wasn't tough and tried to explain,

"Look, the lass was crying, it's Christmas, couldn't you just go and have fun and leave the lasses alone?"

Nope, nothing I said was working and he was still coming for me.

The bus station barriers were there to stop passengers from stepping in front of a bus, there was always an entry and an exit. For some reason, I'll never know why. Although I am incredibly grateful, he didn't come through the exit opening. Seemingly learning to walk upright and walk-through openings was a little too much to grasp in his drunken state.

He came straight to the barrier and stood in front of me. He took a wild swing at me, I stepped back easily making him miss, my back was now against the rail behind me, it would be wrong to think I was suddenly Mohmmad Ali, I was just lucky being out of his drunken reach.

"What if he didn't really want to hurt me?" Was a crazy thought I had.

Wrong, now he climbed up on the bottom rail so he could reach a bit further with his swing, he swung his left wildly and just missed. By now he had figured out how far he could reach, I could see he was leaning almost with his knees on the top rail.

The top rail was about four feet high, with the lower rail on which he stood around two feet off the ground. He now had a height advantage to aim down at me. As his left fist swung past, he was gathering himself for his right to come back at me, the classic drunk haymaker, where you could see the swing originate in the next county before it came anywhere near you. Soon, he would have his range and connect one of these with my head, that was the scenario I wanted to avoid.

By the time (and all of this is in seconds) his right came swinging back around, I had decided I couldn't just stand there and be clobbered, I should defend myself. It would be folly for me to try and hit him; there was no point, he would just laugh, and I would hurt my hand. I reckoned that a better idea would be to defend myself and try to put him on the floor. Reasoning if he was on the floor, he couldn't hurt me, and somebody might come to help me now that some people and some buses were coming into the station.

As his right arm swung, I grabbed a hold and pulled his arm and him over the railing onto the floor in front of me, where he was now flat on his back, and you could see he was genuinely stunned that I wasn't dead and he was the one on the floor. Now, at this point many of you will think I should have stuck the boot in on him while he was down on the floor. I certainly could have kicked him and done him some harm, the problem was he still had two big mates who had yet to become involved, and I was certain they wouldn't stand by and allow me to hurt their mate on the floor. I was now almost crapping myself at the thought of those two jumping in to sort me out.

Oh-oh! My worst fears became real, just as he was hitting the floor, the two big lads who had been standing back now began to move towards where we were.

They came rushing in the entrance to the rails, obviously they were a little smarter than he was, and they had worked out they didn't need to try and climb over the rails. Now I was going to be mincemeat for sure. That was the day I might have invented the moonwalk, three years before Michael Jackson did it, in that moment as I swiftly and seamlessly backed out of the bus stand onto the through fare.

Keeping my eyes on them as they came closer. I thought,

"Not much I can do, I'll try to be defensive, if I turn my back I will definitely be badly hurt!"

They came running up the bus stand and stopped when they got to where he was. Wow, they're helping him to his feet, now the three of them will just come and flatten me for sure. Mentally I was already picking my favourite-coloured straws for my stay in hospital.

We now had several onlookers; I noticed a bus driver or two walking by. A particularly rotund one who must have weighed around 130 kg (around 300 lbs.) was walking past where I was stood and I looked at him pleadingly and said,

"Hey mister, can you do something about this?"

He just looked at me and carried on walking. There were other people in the stands, not one person offered to help me. The two tall lads were arguing with the smaller lad, telling him he was being silly, and looking at me saying,

"He isn't worth it!" They were saying to him.

They were correct, I was nodding in agreement with them 100%.

For a moment, I was feeling quite grateful it looked like they were taking him away back down the bus stand away from me. They had him by the arms, calmly talking to him, about going for another pint, then suddenly, he flung these two bigger lads aside, as if they were just nuisance flies to be swatted away, while yelling,

"He thinks he can have me!" (Which in translation means I am thinking I can beat him in a fight).

I couldn't believe what I was looking at. He turned back towards me and the two lads couldn't hold him, Oh no! Not again? What on earth am I supposed to do if two of his big mates can't even hold him?

He started walking towards me and I naturally started walking backwards, I said,

"I'm not a fighter, I can't fight you and I won't fight you! Obviously you're bigger and tougher than I am and all I wanted was a happy Christmas!"

I continued walking backwards as he came towards me, now only a few feet away.

I couldn't take my eyes off him, I knew that he was drunk, and speed was not his friend, anything he was going to do would be telegraphed and I would be able to get out of the way again. He kept coming towards me, I kept walking backwards. I remember trying to attract the attention of another passing bus driver, still nothing.

I have no idea why he didn't just launch himself at me, he was bigger and clearly could shrug the two big lads off, so hurting me wouldn't have been a challenge. Maybe he wanted me to do something first? Then he could tell the presiding judge that he killed me in self-defence?

Each step backwards I was getting closer to the end of the bus station. He held out his right hand and said,

"Just shake hands then and say, Happy Christmas!"

I smiled and said, "That's okay! Just saying Happy Christmas is enough, thank you!"

He was adamant,

"Nor! You have to say it and shake me hand!" He said in a way I was supposed to take as sincerity.

He wanted me to shake his hand then he would leave. Now, although I wasn't a fighter, I also wasn't completely stupid.

The oldest trick in the book for people wanting to settle a fight is that they ask you to shake hands, then as you reach out to shake hands, they will pull you towards them and then they will head butt you in the face, game over. Somehow, he had decided to go this route instead of just trying to hit me, he must have been really drunk if he thought that me in my alter ego as the skinny snorkel coat fella was a tough guy.

I reached the end of the bus station; I had managed to do a one hundred and eighty and be in the position of going the other way. Walking backwards into the bus station, which thankfully now had even more people.

We could hear police car sirens in the distance, and his two friends began feeling nervous about their Christmas being ruined, and shouted,

"Haway man! Leave him alern, it's not worth it, the coppers might be here soon!"

His two friends were behind me, now I was worried about being sandwiched, walking backwards into them with him in front of me.

His friends shouting about coppers coming seemed to do the trick, suddenly he was anxious just to shake hands and leave. He was a little calmer, almost as if he was going to be an alright kind of guy.

"Right we're gannin ter the pub!" Was the next shout from his friends, "We're off!"

One more time he thrust his hand out and pleaded for me to shake his hand for a happy Christmas, and one more time I politely declined and wished him all the best.

The next thing he just turned, ran and caught up with his friends who were now back where it had all started. They looked as if nothing had happened, off they went on their merry way to the next pub, where I'm sure many a story was told about his bus station adventure that day.

I looked at the people around me and shook my head, surprisingly the rest of my body wasn't shaking, I didn't feel frightened, or brave, just relieved it was all over.

I looked to see if I could see the two girls who I'd become all righteous over. Someone pointed to a bus, I glanced across and saw the two girls sitting on a bus. They both waved, and sort of smiled. A pleased it was over kind of smile, not necessarily a happy Christmas smile, ah the magic of Christmas.

20. MOTORBIKING

My next move was back to Middlesbrough, a change of shoe shops, no more "Tony" now I would be working for "Freeman Hardy Willis." Goodness knows what name the Scottish lads would have made up for me out of that.

I like the town; my mam was born there, and so was my youngest daughter. It certainly has a lot of character and the folks are typically good humoured.

I decided to buy a small motorbike to make the sixteen-mile journey to work. One morning, I cut myself shaving, nothing serious, but those of you who've seen a young man cut himself shaving instantly know that it looks such a mess, with blood spots in a few areas across the face, and always the possibility of the blood getting on your shirt. I just stuck little bits of tissue to cover them until the blood dried.

I still made it to work on time, I was walking through the mall, carrying my crash helmet, feeling quite popular, lots of people smiling at me as I walked past.

"Good morning!" I said to all as I passed the coffee shop.

I got to the shop and walked in, of course being a shoe shop, it had about fifteen full length mirrors. The first thing I saw was me carrying my crash helmet, I had removed my helmet to walk through the mall, sadly I had put the helmet on at home just before I left the house.

I had just walked through the mall with about ten bits of bloody red toilet tissue stuck to various parts of my face, with loads of people staring at me.

There I was thinking I was Mr. Popular, with everyone smiling and grinning at me, while all the while I looked like someone who had just been allowed out of the asylum for a day, with bloody red bits of blotchy tissue paper stuck to my face.

In future before donning said crash helmet I would be sure to look in the mirror at home first.

I had bought the motorbike thinking this would be the solution to all my commuting problems, the truth is, I had problems with the motorbike, I should never have gone motorbike shopping on my own, the poor little thing had a tragic gasket problem and oil was always leaking. Every time I had to fill up I also had to fill the oil up. I was what people in the know when it comes to buying vehicles would call,

"A complete berk!"

One morning I couldn't fix the oil leak, but I was "lucky enough" to borrow a small step through Honda 90. I should have just stayed at home.

Part of the journey was down the A19, a major dual carriageway with a speed limit of seventy miles per hour, filled with eighteen-wheel lorries and cars driving crazily.

I'm sure drivers must have been howling with laughter at me travelling like Evel Knievel on a Honda 90 step through, in my pin stripe suit and powder blue crash hat.

I used to try to get behind a lorry, because their speeds were restricted to fifty-five mile per hour, which meant at full throttle I could just about stay in their wind-stream. Looking back, I must have been braver than I thought or completely insane.

Nor was the Honda 90 designed for such a rigorous journey and after repeated "borrowing" it was no surprise that the Honda 90 finally gave out. I couldn't get it on a bus, so I called my dad. He lived about forty-five minutes from where I'd conked out.

"Er hi dad! Yes it's me, I'm stuck with a broken-down Honda 90 on the A174 by Normamby. No I don't have a Honda 90, I borrowed it, no I don't know what's wrong with it but it won't go and I don't have anything to even pretend I can fix it. Okay I guess I'll wait here then and see you in an hour, thanks!"

Dad came and rescued me, we should have left it by the roadside, instead we ended up throwing it in the boot. What about that! My transportation to work fit in the boot of a SAAB.

Top tip, if your commute to work is a choice between walking, taking the bus, quitting the job or riding a moped down a major highway, I would select any one of the first three, but definitely never again would I decide to buy a small motorcycle or ride a moped or motor scooter in busy traffic.

21. A-HOLE

As a retail manager, sometimes you must be an arsehole, you don't want to be, and it still rankles that I did it, but it had the desired effect.

Shops used to have beautiful ornate fascia (the sign above the shop). These signs used to be stainless steel or glass and would light up or look magnificent in the dark with the window lights on. Trouble was, they always needed cleaning.

We were paying a window cleaner to clean them, but we weren't sure that he was doing it properly. We would challenge the window cleaner on pay day and he would say that he came at 6am before we were anywhere near the building. I called a friend, who'd worked in retail since Dickensian times for some advice on how to prove if they were being done or not.

"Hey Pete, yeah it's me Ben. You know I've got a window cleaner comes before anyone is here, he charges us ten quid for doing the fascia, but it never really looks very sparkly, how can I tell if he touches it or not?"

"Oh that's an easy one!" Laughed Pete down the phone, "just go above the fascia, and put a coin on top, if the coin is wiped off you know he's done a thorough job, if it's still there after he says he's been, then you know they just threw some water at it ha-ha!"

"Oh right! Cheers!" I said, "That sounds a bit devious, a bit cunning, but I bet it works ha-ha!"

As luck would have it, above the fascia was a big old sash window which opened. I could lean out and drop a coin on top of the first letter of the fascia. Each morning I went upstairs and looked out of the window and there was the coin sitting nicely staring back at me, already beginning to get a dust ring around it.

I thought of it as more of a silly game than being an a-hole at the time, but when the window cleaner came in on Friday morning for his money, I definitely sounded like an a-hole.

"Good morning! Ah yes, your bill for cleaning the windows, and does that include the cleaning of the fascia?" I asked in a manner not too dissimilar to a crazy Basil Fawlty from "Fawlty Towers" which was often repeated on our television screens.

"Ur yes!" Was the puzzled reply from my window cleaner. He did stop short of saying, "What a stupid question, you skinny moron, it clearly states on the bill and it's the same bill every week!"

"Ah right," I continued, "In that case I would like you to follow me!" There I was beckoning this fully grown adult window cleaner to follow me through the stockroom and up the stairs, like he was a naughty schoolboy.

I opened the window and pointed to my coin sitting on top of the fascia.

"See!" I declared, like some victorious general pointing to a land I just laid waste to. "I placed this coin on the top last week, and it's still there!" I stopped short of saying "A-ha!" I continued, "If indeed you had cleaned the whole fascia correctly then that would have been cleaned away!"

The window cleaner peered out, saw the coin, reached out, picked it up, handed it to me and said,

"There you are, now it's gone! If yer going to be an arsehole about stuff I'm not sure I wanna clean yer windows, and being as I'm the cleaner for the town, and nobody would move in on my patch, that means yerd be cleaning yer arn windows!"

Looking back his reply was much kinder than just throwing me out of the window.

He continued, "Now if yer not happy with any of the work I'm doing just say so or point ter summit and ask if I can mek sure it's done proper, none of this stupid nonsense about hiding stuff in places to see if anyone cleans!" Then he started to smile as he turned to walk back downstairs, he finished with, "Eee is that what they are training managers these days ha-ha!"

I called Pete back, "Hey Pete!" I said, "That thing with the coin worked, cheers, though you never told me I'd be a bit of a dick if I actually did it!"

"Ha-ha!" Pete laughed down the phone, "Well it's all part of being a manager, just one of the tools of the trade."

"Yeah but I wish I'd just said summit to the fella!"

"Nar," He said, "It's much more fun, besides when you get more staff you haven't got time to be chasing after everyone who's not doing something right. Do the same thing with the staff inside, stick a coin on top of the mirrors, use a washable marker in the corner of the mirrors to make sure they're cleaning properly!"

"Oh my goodness! Ha-ha!" I laughed, "You really do lay all these little traps out to see if they're all cleaning properly!"

"Ha-ha! Yeah!" He continued, "but whatever you do, don't try doing that at home!"

We both laughed at the thought of going home and putting pennies on top of pictures or mirrors, then our spouses would surely beat us with the said pictures or mirrors ha-ha.

Seemingly I passed the a-hole training, and I certainly learned to have more respect for people working around me, the window cleaner forgave me and would laugh about it for a long time afterwards.

In future, I wouldn't set any more traps, or play any tricks, preferring to just speak as I find and tell people the things I thought they hadn't done.

I was wrong, as a retail manager, or any manager you must never be an arsehole.

22. 1984

The year was 1984, Orwellian enough in reality, employment and living standards where I lived were being affected by the coal miners' strike. To stay in a job, I ended up being transferred to a shop at Whitehaven.

As we drove in, I remember my father stating,

"If you took the cars off the streets, it would look exactly the same as it did in 1952!"

That was the year when he was last there doing a study of a decaying society due to changes in economic demand. Whitehaven had a history of being a busy ship trading port, but sadly had no longer been a busy anything for about sixty years.

The shop I had to manage was on King St, right in the middle of the town. Every morning just before 9 a.m. the old delivery van belonging to the shop next door would be parked across the entrance to my shop doorway. The driver Trevor was a big lad, over six-foot-tall and close to seventeen stone (over 107 Kilos in weight).

And every morning I would go out shaking my head, tut tutting like a Mr. Rigsby in "Rising Damp" laughing at the lads saying,

"Haway man! Get this blooming heap shifted, I've got to have customers coming in!"

They would in turn grin back at me, disappear into the carpet shop, from whence Trev would emerge and say,

"Oh can they not get past it like?"

"No! And you know fine well, we do this every morning, I swear one day I should just let your tires down, ha-ha!"

"Whey, then it'll never move, will it?" He'd say laughing, as he hopped in and moved it twelve feet back in front of the carpet shop.

This went on for months, sometimes they'd get there at 8 am and be out of the way before we opened, but a few times a week, we'd play out this charade.

The owner of the carpet shop was a gentle humble man and he would always be apologetic, as soon as the van had driven off to make his deliveries he would usually come into my shop and say,

"I always tell him (Trev) not to park there. I hope he didn't cause you any problems!"

I would always laugh and reassure him,

"It's all good, Trevor's a good guy, and I know he's just trying to line the back of his van up with your front door."

Perhaps he thought that the big company I worked for might try to make life awkward for his personally owned shop, but I would never say anything to anyone else except him and Trevor.

Just before Christmas, Trevor and Billy his number two came straight into my shop laughing and said,

"Look Ben, we're parking in front for ten minutes and we don't want to hear you complain!"

I laughed and said,

"Well if you park your rust bucket out front, don't blame me if it gets towed away! I'll be sure to split the scrap value with you tho!"

My response was exactly what they had hoped for, and with a big grin on both of their faces, Trevor and Billy marched behind my sales counter.

"We think it's time we showed you what happens to people who are cheeky to their elders!" They said as they took hold of me.

Either one of them was big enough to hold me, and it was Billy who held my hands behind my back, while Trevor with his big laugh, asked around the customers and staff who were all watching and highly amused,

"Shall we?" While he held his carpet scissors in his right hand and pulled my tie outwards with his left hand.

"Yes! Yes! Ha-ha!" Was the unanimous response from staff and customers alike, all of them obviously in the festive spirit of "Get the Boss!"

Of course I was giggling too, even though my laughter might have been more of a nervous nature, despite Trevor having a pair of carpet scissors waving around in front of me, the situation was funny.

Trevor took his carpet scissors and basically shredded my tie from the base to about two inches from the top, then laughing louder both he and Billy disappeared to their shop next door

Two minutes later the owner of the next-door shop came running in,

"Oh no!" He apologised profusely, "I'm so sorry, so sorry, I told them not to do anything!"

Trevor and Billy had been laughing so hard when they went next door that they had to tell him.

"It's okay!" I said laughing, "Everyone enjoyed it, the staff have been hoping for something like that for ages, and besides I never liked that tie anyway."

To try and make amends, the owner invited me to his shop's staff Christmas party, that weekend. Of course I accepted and naturally I was seated next to Trevor.

When Trevor went to the toilet, one of Trevor's co-workers said to me,

"You know, every year at these parties our owner has a professional photographer come in and take a team picture."

"Ah sounds like a good idea."

"Yeah, and for the photo, he likes all of the men to wear a tie."

"Ha-ha! Yeah, yeah, you heard about the tie thing then?"

"Of course," they continued, "but the main thing is Brian hates wearing ties, and he isn't wearing one at the moment. He always brings one to wear just for the photo then he takes it back off after the photo. His tie is there in the pocket of his jacket on the chair beside you."

"So let me get this straight!" I said with a big grin, "Brian has his tie, ready to put on just for the picture. And it's in this pocket beside me?"

"You got it!" They said,

Finding a pair of scissors wasn't difficult, I quickly located the tie in the jacket pocket, and while laughing, before Trevor made it back from the toilet, I shredded his tie into many small pieces.

After we had eaten, Trevor's boss, the carpet shop owner called us to order,

"Come on everyone, look smart, we're going to have a picture taken."

The room fell apart as Trevor put his jacket on, put his hand in his pocket and pulled out the pieces of his tie. Trevor looked at me, gave a huge grin and gave me a bear hug that almost took my last breath. Not that I minded, as I was too busy laughing with the rest of them.

From what I would later learn there weren't many people who would try to pull a practical joke on Trevor.

I had certainly had a more colourful 1984 than Mr. Orwell would have predicted.

23. THE BOXER

I started going out for a drink or two after work with Trevor, some of the shopfitters working on the shop came along one night and we all went to the local nightclub.

Naturally you get barged about a little in a small club that's packed, and one such incident occurred to knock my drink a little.

I turned and shouted over the music to the lad who had barged me,

"Hoo man! Watch what you're doing!" Not that I was feeling tough, it was just a natural knee jerk reaction if someone ever "spilled" your pint.

The lad turned around as if to challenge me, as far as I was concerned, protocol in a bar when spilling a drink was at least to offer to replace it, even if I wouldn't want him to.

He glared at me, reminding me a little of the troll I'd seen at the bus station in Hartlepool, seemingly just about to tell me where to go when the words that came out of his mouth were,

"Oh, soz! Erm, would you like another pint?"

"Nah! I'm good thanks." I replied, pleased that at least he'd acknowledged he was in the wrong.

The night carried on and I never gave it another thought till the next day, when all the shopfitters were talking with Kathleen, the shop supervisor, who also knew everyone in the town.

"I hear you went out with Trevor last night!" She said,

"Oh aye," I said, "we had a canny night, went to a nightclub anarl!"

The shopfitters started laughing, one of them said,

"Aye, you should have seen him, Ben was acting all tough, nearly got himself into a fight, till the lad clocked eyes on Trevor, then shit hissell and apologised, meanwhile, Ben here was thinking he was all tough!"

The rest of the group fell about laughing, each remembering me challenging the lad who had knocked me beer in my hand.

"No way ha-ha!" I said laughing along with them, "besides why would he care that Trevor was there?"

I was always guilty of never appreciating how other people react around tough guys, to me everyone was just the same as me, well not as puny as I was, or cursed with the same inability to fight, but apart from that generally just like me.

Now Kathleen started laughing, and she said,

"Oh my goodness, ha-ha! Yer a silly bugger! Everyone in the town who ever went out for a drink knows who Trevor is, ha-ha! He has been the doorman at all the nightclubs and pubs and he used to be a heavyweight boxer!"

"Well duh!" I said, "You could've told me, I mean I've been giving him a hard time since the first time I met him, I always thought he was just a big, nice guy ha-ha!"

They were all laughing, explaining to me that's how I'd been walking around the town without anyone ever bothering me.

When you stood back and looked at Trevor it made sense, some of our nights out together now made more sense too.

Next time we went out for a drink, I mentioned, or rather asked Trevor,

"So how come, you never told me you were an ex-boxer and a doorman?"

His reply was priceless and a great lesson for everyone. He said,

"Nobody in this town and I mean nobody, talks to me the way you do! You take the piss and treat me the same as you do everyone else, normal, and I love it! Most people fear my past reputation but to you it doesn't matter! So I'd appreciate it if you just carried on!" As he gave me one of his famous bear hugs, with a big grin on his face.

I was rather chuffed that night. Treat everyone the same, old, young, rich, poor, tough, or mean, everyone just really wants to have friends.

24. SHORT BUS TRIP

Local accents in the U.K. are always fascinating. You can travel three miles and the way people say things immediately change.

Getting on a bus in Cumbria, we were going from Whitehaven to Aspatria. I was from the Northeast of England, where there are very broad and varied accents, but was now living on the Northwest coast, where the words were corrupted even further.

I said to the driver, "Two to Aspatria please!"

Now I'm sure many of you are reading this are saying "Aspatria?" Saying it as you see it, Ass pate rea, and that is exactly how I said it.

The driver looked at me all kind of funny, and replied, "Wat?"

I repeated, "Two to Aspatria please!" This time speaking slowly and emphasizing my annunciation, "Ah – Spay – Tree- Arr!"

The driver looked beyond me, to the line of people behind me, I figured looking for clues, to help him I showed him the address I was traveling to in Aspatria, which luckily I had written down before leaving home.

The penny dropped for him, as he exclaimed with a big smile, "Oh! Thu means Spatry, Spat – Tree!"

"Yes!" I laughed out, "I guess we mean Spatry."

25. TROLLEY TRIP

Whitehaven, had loads of great small bars in the 1980's. As a result, we would often find ourselves leaving some watering hole and staggering towards our homes at 2am.

Some kind soul had left a shopping trolley just outside the pub. We decided it would be funny if we each took turns sitting in the shopping trolley, while the other pushed as we sang silly songs and made funny race car noises all the way home.

Not surprisingly at 2:30am, the streets were quiet, and for the most part we went through the back streets avoiding any main roads.

As we emerged from the shadows of one alley, there was one main road to cross. If we made it across this road in one piece without detection, we were home and dry. At the top of the next alley was a hotel.

Dazza lived opposite the hotel, and this was our agreed stopping point with the shopping cart.

We decided an empty shopping cart would be easier to run across the road with, and I promptly jumped out. We looked left, looked right, looking for police cars. No sign of anything.

This was perfect, we dashed across the road, giggling, as we made it back into the next back alley behind the main road, so dark that once you were in the shadows you couldn't be seen. This time Dazza jumped in, and we carried on with silly songs and noises.

At the top of the alley, was the front of the hotel, and with a mighty last push I thrust Dazza and the shopping cart back into the bright glare of the street lighting, almost bumping into a parked car.

Yup, it was a police car.

This is one of those moments when you sober up quickly and remember that even though you're acting like a ten-year-old, one of you is supposed to be a manager and the other employed by the government.

The two officers sat in the car started grinning, we were thinking about the local news headlines flashing before us,

"Manager Caught drunk in charge of shopping cart!" Or "Government worker too drunk to walk steals shopping cart!"

At least I wasn't in the shopping cart. I'm sure the sight of Dazza sat knees to his chest had something to do with their grins.

The two police officers wound their car windows down, Dazza thought humour was our best form of defence, as he asked the policemen in his sarcastic Liverpool accent,

"Do you lads wanna have a gow?"

They laughed, shook their heads and asked,

"Now then lads, where did you find the trolley?"

"Well, we just kind of saw it back in town!" Said Dazza, looking for sympathy from the two officers.

"Okay then! If you take it back to exactly where you found it we'll say no more about it!" Said the driver.

"Oh, and lads!" Said the second cop, "No more riding in it, just take the empty trolley back nicely!"

We obviously didn't look like criminals. The police were great.

Though there's nothing quite like having to walk an extra two miles at 2:30am in the morning to help sober you up.

We were tempted to leave it halfway back, that thought quickly disappeared when the police car slowly drove past us, with two policemen laughing and pointing at us, just to remind us that they were watching our every move.

Yup, living in a quiet town was fun, but there wasn't much you could do that would go unnoticed.

26. HOOK LINE AND SINKER

Keeping with the theme of never staying anywhere for too long, I moved to Alnwick, in Northumberland, (pronounced Annik not Aileen week). An old English market town, where I believe they filmed Harry Potter and Robin Hood, among other movies, using parts of the town or castle as a backdrop.

The shop was brand new in the town, as was I, so I didn't know much about local stuff, except of course they had a big castle ha-ha!

While we were setting the shop up, getting ready to open, Hazel one of the employees who had lived local all her life asked me,

"Hey boss! What are we doing for the Alnwick Fair?"

"Huh! What's Alnwick Fair?" Was my puzzled response.

"Call yourself a northerner, and you have never heard of Alnwick Fair! Ha-ha!" Hazel joked.

"Nope, honestly I've never heard of it ha-ha!"

Hazel continued, "Every year, there is a weeklong medieval fair, where locals dress up in medieval outfits and take part in town events, like the wench dunking, the throwing of wet sponges at people in the stocks, live music, the opening parade and a barbecue in the market square."

"Oh, sounds excellent," I said, "What kind of things do you think we should do?"

"Well, get the staff to dress up that week and we can all do the opening day parade."

"Great idea, that'll be good publicity, especially if we are advertising the shop name ha-ha! Let me see if I can get some money from the company to pay for costumes."

"Yeah, you'd better be quick," Hazel urged, "The costume hire companies will soon be busy and it's only about eight weeks or so till it starts in June."

The district manager agreed to give me two hundred quid as long as the staff wore some sashes during the parade and I got some photos he could send to the company magazine.

All the staff agreed to dress up and take part in the opening day parade and then continue to wear the costume at work for the rest of the week. I chose the most suitable costume for me; the red and green jester's outfit complete with a three-pointed floppy jester's hat and a bell at the end of each point. With a little jig in my step, I managed to annoy the group of Morris Dancers who were in the parade in front of me, as we marched around the town.

Each day, the "Medieval Militia" would hold events to entertain members of the public. The most popular event happened each lunchtime, when the militia would court martial "a wench" and subsequently tie her to a stool to be plunged, fully clothed into a water filled skip.

Naturally, I said to the militia,

"If you find yourselves a bit short of suitable wenches to dunk in the water, there is always one we can spare from the shop."

Twice during the week the militia came bounding into the shop and escorted one of the employees to be court martialled and publicly dunked in the market square.

We had a great week, loads of laughs, and certainly for a new shop that made ourselves noticed in the town, which I regarded as important because the town had many old traditions and didn't always welcome bigger retail companies to the party.

At the end of the week on Friday at 4 p.m., I received a telephone call at work.

"Hello, Can I speak to the manager please?"

"Yes! This is him speaking, how can I help you?"

"This is the local Newspaper, The Gazette! We wanted to congratulate you on your participation in this year's annual medieval festival!"

"Oh, thank you, we really enjoyed it!"

The voice on the phone continued, "Well each year, we pick the three best participant stores in the town and write a small feature article, complete with pictures, to not only show our appreciation, but also provide you with a little free publicity and it's a feel-good story. As one of the winners, you also qualify for a free meal at The White Swan Hotel for you and your staff, where we can take some more pictures! Does that sound like something you would be able to accept, or do we have to pick a different winner?"

"Wow, yes that sounds brilliant! What do we have to do?"

"On Monday morning, just call the Gazette office and ask for 'Dave the Events Manager' and let him know the number of people who will be attending the free meal on Wednesday."

"Oh wow, that's excellent, thank you. What is the best number?"

He gave me a number and I was so excited as we said our goodbyes, that as soon as I put the phone down, I called my regional manager to brag about our success. Not very humble in my youth, I couldn't wait for him to tell me how excellent we all were. Especially as he had raised his eyebrows at spending £200 on fancy dress outfits.

Dang! He wasn't in, I relayed the story to his secretary, I was so excited, even jumping up and down animatedly on the phone while telling her all the best bits of the week and how great the staff had been in participating, how we were going to be in the local newspaper, and how we had a free meal at the local top hotel.

The shop telephone was beside the cash register, and as I put the phone down, Eileen another one of the ladies working for me, said,

"Sorry! I couldn't help overhearing!"

Eileen continued, "Did you get the name of the person you were speaking to?"

"Sorry no!" I replied, "He just said to call Dave the events manager on Monday!"

"Oh no!" She replied with a shocked look on her face.

"What's wrong?" I asked.

"Well," Eileen said, "you know how "Tab" (her husband) likes to play practical jokes?"

"Yes, ha-ha!" I agreed laughing, "I do know how Tab liked to play practical jokes."

"Well," continued Eileen, "they (The Gazette) don't have prizes for the best dressed shop!"

Eileen had lived in the town since birth, and emphasised,

"The Gazette certainly doesn't spring for a free meal for anyone in this town! They don't have that kind of money ha-ha! And did anyone come into the shop talking about the participation either before, during or after the event started?"

"Erm no! I don't think so." Of course I knew they hadn't. "Oh no!" The cogs were whirling in my mind, the penny finally dropped for me, I looked at Eileen, "That must mean, Oh no! Tab's just got me good and proper, hasn't he!"

Laugh, cry, faint, scream, all the above, I just want the ground to open and swallow me.

Trouble is my boss wasn't noted for his sense of humour, a rumour ran around the company for years that he had fired his own sister for taking a Saturday off to go to her own wedding.

Talk about Basil Fawlty, as I stood thrashing the shelves in front of me with my notes about the prize we hadn't won.

I called the regional managers office straight back, his secretary answered,

"You know I just called to say we won a prize with the local Gazette for Alnwick Fair Week? Did you get to tell the district manager anything yet? No? Ah thank goodness! Phew! Erm well, we didn't win anything, and the whole thing was a complete misunderstanding by me, there would in fact be no meal, no photographs, no free publicity, and no prize!

Thanks Tab! You got me hook line and sinker.

Below a picture of me in full Jester outfit.

Below caught harassing the "Morris Dancers" in front of me.

27. WHEN A HORSE FARTS

I used to get a bus in from an exceedingly small village, Bilton, into Alnwick. Each morning, I would walk to the bus stop. Down the pretty village lane, past the small shop and post office, over a small stone bridge which crossed the rail tracks, with a six-foot stone wall on my left-hand side.

Saturday mornings were always quiet and devoid of any other human activity. Each Saturday, I would be the only one walking down the lane and the only one getting on at this bus stop.

On one beautiful Spring Saturday morning, the air was so fresh, so English, I was walking towards the bridge, noticing the buds on the flowers, the bees buzzing by, the birds singing in the air. I was walking along the bridge feeling lucky to be enjoying such a morning.

The only real problem was I had been out drinking the night before. Just as I got to the end of the bridge, I exploded a beer fart a horse would have been proud of, think of the longest noisiest fart you ever heard, even if it was on television, then double it.

This was a sound barrier breaker, long and thunderous, you could hear my cheeks rattling. You could feel the bridge rattling, and hear windows a few streets away rattling, completely defying the logic of the universe that such a noise could be wrested from a human. I needed that, now I felt great, I exhaled and exclaimed at the same time a feeling of relief, relief that it was out and I hadn't shat myself, but still relief.

"Ahhhhhhhhh!" I proudly exclaimed.

All that gas exploding into the atmosphere, exactly as I am stepping off the end of the bridge, past the end of the six-foot stone wall. That morning, standing waiting for the one and only time in the history of all Saturday mornings in the entire history of the village, was a sweet middle-aged lady. We never did make eye contact.

Being raised as a repressed farter, usually meant that any farts I did were not directly attributable to me. The best example of this happened one evening walking to a footy game at Roker Park.

I always went to the games with "Big Tom." We came to a road to cross, and I was going to fart. Walking along in a crowd is normally fine because nobody has a clue who is responsible, but here we were, standing in a small group waiting for the police to give us the "okay" to cross the road.

Just as we stopped I released a "Silent But Deadly" (SBD). I waited for the abuse to come from those around us, surely it wouldn't take much of a Columbo to realise that I was the culprit.

Being of slight build, okay skinny, certainly had advantages, because the smell that emanated from my decaying insides that evening clearly proved too monstrous for anyone to believe that such a heinous reeking guffing stench could possibly come from one so slight.

At the same time, there was a mounted policeman trotting by on the road in front of us and my theory was confirmed when big Tom said,

"Cor smell that fuckin reeking horse!"

With everyone around us, making suitable noises in agreement, along the lines of,

"Bur-yak! That's fuckin disgusting!" While putting their scarves in front of their noses.

I guess I could have claimed it, after all there can't be too many people out there whose farts smell so bad that they could pass off as horse fart's.

If the sweet little old lady is reading this, I am apologising a little late, I hope it didn't ruin your day. Also to all the people I worked with in confined retail spaces, especially those behind the cash desk in the small shops, though I like to think I became quite good at pulling faces to indicate that it wasn't me and I was blaming someone else at the time.

28. A QUICK INTERVIEW

I had an interview with Campbell's, a well-known food producer/manufacturer. The job was for a line manager at a factory near Peterborough, a long way from where I lived.

I had no factory experience, no food experience, but I am enthusiastic, and my managerial experience must have impressed them.

After reviewing my application and C.V. Campbell's paid for a three-hour train ride to the interview, and if I was successful would have meant a new start earning more money and moving to pastures new.

Unlike my earlier interviews, my travel to and from the location was completely unremarkable, I'd like to think by this time of life I'd remembered to go to bed early, set an alarm and make the appointment on time.

The interviewer showed me around the factory, explaining in great detail the process, and how the lines worked to me, then he asked me,

"What do you know about Campbell's?"

This was my chance to shine, a smart person would have regaled him with how much they knew about the one hundred plus year history of the global brand, not me, all I could muster was,

"Oh yeah!" I volunteered, "Campbell's the ones who make the thick soups!"

I meant to say condensed and then elaborate on my knowledge of their invention and expansion into global markets.

Sadly, once again I'd shot myself in the foot, and I wasn't destined to become the "man in charge of the can."

You could tell he'd heard enough. As it turns out, thick soups are only a small part of their repertoire, and on that day, I felt thicker than any soup they had ever made.

It was a long way to go for such a short interview, still, at least I was having interview practice.

29. FERAL

Back to working in Alnwick, where I had my worst experience with wild animals, feral cats to be precise. You might not want to read this section if you are a little squeamish or just don't like sad animal stories. It took me a whole fifteen years before I could be close to a cat again.

One morning, everyone kept hearing sounds like a cat wailing, coming from the walls of the shop. Actually, it wasn't like a cat wailing; it was a cat wailing.

We traced the sound to the front of the shop. Turns out the noise wasn't from the walls, the noise was from the roof above us, in the attic above the shop windows.

I had never been up there; I didn't want to go up there. Luckily, by now, life's lessons were beginning to take effect and I had learned to work well with the window cleaner and stop trying to be a "clever arse!" His name was Handy Al, a do anything you want kind of bloke. His main thing was cleaning windows and he helped many of the owner-occupied retail outlets with odd jobs.

I had a quick chat with Handy Al,

"Hey Al, would you be able to take a look up in that front loft section of the shop?"

"Ha-ha! Just because you're scared to go up!" he laughed.

"Well maybe." I smiled.

"The girls (staff) already told me about the noises and said you might ask me ha-ha!"

Al grabbed one of the taller stockroom ladders and went to the power cupboard behind the shop windows where the loft hatch was.

There was only a small loft above the front windows for appearances on the street, the rest of the roof behind the front windows was all flat.

I waited at the bottom of the ladder while he first moved the hatch, then popped his head up, then climbed up.

"Oh, oh!" He shouted down to me.

"What is it?" I asked, wondering if I had to run for my life or continue holding the ladder for him.

There was a little kerfuffle, and then Al came back to the hatch and back down the ladder.

"You're gonna need to call animal welfare." He said.

"What did you see?" I asked.

"Well, there's a big feral cat and I can't get close, as soon as I got near, it ran through a hole in the back of your roof, so when you catch it, you'll need to call that in to be fixed!"

"Oh is that all?" I suddenly felt better that it wasn't a wild bear or crazy kangaroo, although neither were in the wild in England, you never can be too sure. "Okay," I continued, "I'll call animal welfare straight away."

A quick call revealed that they would indeed come and collect the feral cat; they wouldn't, however, come and chase it around a loft until they had caught it. They would give me traps I could set up in the loft and catch the feral cat without being mauled to death in the process.

Excellent, they brought the trap and Handy Al was kind enough to place it in the loft. Now, all we had to do was go home and come back in the morning, see the cat in the cage and call the animal people who would then come and take the cat away.

The next morning, Handy Al had even hurried his rounds up so that he could go up and get the cat as soon as I arrived at work. He came down grinning with a large feral cat in the cage. Then, he told me there was an additional problem.

"You better call animal welfare back, there's another four kittens up there!"

I hadn't counted on that. A quick call to the animal welfare people and they said if we could put the kittens in a box, they would take them also.

Well, being a shoe shop, boxes weren't hard to come by ha-ha!

Once again Handy Al went into the breach, well the loft, and this time he came down with a box of kittens. Everybody in the shop said, "Ahhhhhh!"

We put the kittens in the back of the stockroom close to mommy cat. We suddenly thought some people might want a kitten to take home, after all mom cat was feral, but these cute little kittens didn't know what they were yet.

A few of us went to look at the cute kittens. When we were looking at the kittens, we noticed that some of their eyes seemed sealed shut, due to eyes running then becoming congealed.

I called the animal welfare to ask if they had seen anything like this? They told me it might be cat flu, often common in feral cats, and that if I wanted, I could try to assist one of the kittens by trying gently to help open an eye. Spoiler alert! Don't try this at home.

As I was gently trying to open the eye, it squirted fluid out! And I'm sure it made a popping sound! Oh! My goodness I had just popped the poor kitten's eye. I jumped back, the girls screamed, or was it the other way around? Handy Al left. The poor kittens had a form of cat flu.

Oh no! As I'm writing this, I'm getting those bad feelings again. I felt terrible for ages, I still feel terrible. It was the worst thing I have voluntarily done, and one which gave me nightmares about cats for a long time.

In the last twenty years, I've had three cats, the last one even a feral rescue, which makes me hope and believe that the feline population of this world has forgiven me. Sadly, the kittens were indeed taken away by the animal shelter. I never did follow up with them.

30. NICKNAMES

I started working in the insurance industry. At the time regular working people still paid for insurance policies with cash or a check. To accommodate regular payments the insurance companies hired agents to go door to door and collect payments, do claims administration and sell new policies.

Other industries providing products and services to consumers also had to collect cash or check payments from houses door to door. Friday was still traditionally pay day for working men and women. This made Friday a busy day for householders to pay bills and if you looked closely at many small towns and villages in the UK on Friday afternoons, you would have seen wandering between houses, crisscrossing the streets, the rent man, the potato man, the coupon man, the milkman, the window cleaner, the tally man and the insurance man.

I'd like to think that as an Insurance man we occupied a special place; for example, in some houses, we were trusted to knock and walk straight in, the money and payment book usually on the kitchen table, or the mantelpiece above the fire, we would record the entry, take the money and leave.

I worked alongside many characters, some more memorable than others.

Buster got his name, because when he lost his temper, his head would turn purple and he'd start shouting,

"I'm gonna bust thu lad!"

Though as far as I can remember he never even bust a pimple.

Budgie got his name because he was always chirpy, chipping in with answers when nobody even had a question.

Turvey got his name because he looked like English comedian Rik Mayall, who had a character called Kevin Turvey, and also became famous as part of "The Young Ones."

Then there was Para, let me tell you how Para got his nickname.

Para knocked and walked into a house one day. A small house, a bungalow. The elderly occupant was nowhere to be seen.

The money and payment book were on the kitchen table. Our usual modus operandi was to take the money, mark the payment book and leave.

Instead of marking the payment book and leaving, Para poked his head into the front room to see if anyone was home. He didn't see anyone becoming concerned and decided to look a little further.

A door in the corner of the front room led to the bedroom. Lying on the bed was the old lady who lived there.

Para had already gone further than most of us ever would have dared. Instead of just leaving or shouting from the kitchen,

"Thank you, see you next week!"

Para decided to call the police and ambulance.

Oh yeah, the lady was thrilled to be woken from her afternoon nap by the local emergency services.

That's when we decided to call him Para, short for paramedic.

Picture below, "we always had fun selling insurance."

31. PLEASE DON'T GO

Training courses are a necessary evil! Always memorable, not for the training, mainly for the out of hours activities when you're away from home, in a hotel, in a big city on the company dime. This one instance I went out with Mark in Leeds. Midweek to a nightclub, it was quiet but at least we had a few late drinks to prepare us for the next day. We got back to the hotel, giggling, eating kebabs, we were just about to call it a night, when we saw Tony in the hall in front of us heading to his room with a girl he had met at the nightclub.

As Tony and the girl approached his room, we could tell by the conversation and her body language that she didn't really want to go in with him, she was okay laughing and chatting, but we could hear her saying,

"No, not tonight!" Every time he mentioned going to his room.

As soon as Tony saw us, he changed his tack,

"Well at least let's go in the room out of the way of those two so we can talk about it! He said, sounding almost like he was pleading with her not to stand in the corridor for us to see.

"Okay!" She agreed with him or relented depending on whose side of the story you're telling.

A big hotel, with armchairs in the hallways outside the bedroom doors. Naturally, Mark and I mischievously plonked down outside his room, where we knew we would be able to hear Tony's "sales technique." There we sat, finishing our kebabs, grinning to each other, sensing this story wasn't over yet.

We could hear muffled voices, so we decided as soon as we finished our kebabs, to get out of the seats, and get closer to the door in order to hear better. Okay I'll admit to it, we placed our ears to his door, but who can remember the finer details. I'll never know how we didn't fall through the door laughing as we heard him begging her to please stay the night with him, he would even sleep on the chair and she could have the bed all to herself, just if she stayed and didn't leave him. Well, that did it, Mark and I were absolutely rolling around laughing on the floor of the corridor. The conversation we overheard went something like this.

Him, "Please stay! You can have the bed and I'll sleep on the sofa!"

Her, "No, I really don't want to spend the night."

Him, "But, please, I promise I won't do anything!"

Her, "Nah that's okay, I really just don't want to."

Him, "Well how about just sitting here with me for an hour having a drink and watching something on TV?"

Her, "No, I really think I must be going!"

Him, "Please, please, please don't go!"

Her, "Sorry, it's late and I must head home."

Him, "Please, please, please don't go!"

Her, "I'm not staying!"

Him, "Well I can get my car and give you a ride home."

Her, "No that's ok thank you, I'll go downstairs and get a taxi."

I nudged Mark, we moved away from the door, we sensed she was about to exit, we dodged into the doorway of my room, which was conveniently next door.

We were both giggling as she was coming out of his room and we could still hear him pleading, he must have been on his knees by this time, then he closed his door. We watched her walk to the elevator, and I turned to Mark and whispered,

"Quick, follow me!"

Mark was curious, and by the time we got to the elevator, we had formulated a little plan. First, we made sure the elevator had gone all the way down, so that we knew the girl had left the hotel, then the fun could begin.

We waited about ninety seconds then went back and knocked on Tony's door.

Poor Tony, he must have thought it was the girl changing her mind and coming back. The door opened before the second knock even connected.

The door swung open, Tony was wearing nothing but his shiny white Y-fronts and a great big smile, which slid off his face like cold custard, as soon as he saw it was only Mark and me. We chose to ignore his attire, and asked him,

"Wasn't that pretty girl with the long dark hair and black dress with you?"

Tony replied, indignantly, "Yes, but she's gone! Why? What do you want to know for?"

I smiled and replied, "Oh, we just saw her in the lobby looking for a taxi, I told her I would get my car keys and give her a ride home!"

Mark added a knowing wink and nodded in agreement saying, "I'm surprised you let that one slip Tony!"

Tony leapt into action, and in one move he had spun around, grabbed his trousers, shirt, and car keys exclaiming to us in his doorway,

"Oh no you're not! She's mine! I'll be the one to take her home!"

"Well, if you're sure?" I replied, "I mean I don't wanna fight about it, but you'd better hurry, she's waiting just outside the main doors."

Within a second or two, Tony had passed us in the doorway, still fastening the buttons on his shirt, thanking us profusely for letting him know, impatiently tapping the elevator button and smiling back at us.

As soon as Tony was on the elevator, Mark and I once again fell in a heap on the floor, rolling around and laughing.

We would just look at each other, at look at Tony's door, then together we would get on our knees and mimic Tony saying,

"Please don't go!"

Then glance down the corridor towards the elevator and start laughing all over again.

Only a few minutes had elapsed when the elevator bell sounded again, Tony re-emerged from the elevator with one of those looks and a poise that can only be described as a week-old deflated balloon.

He asked us,

"Are you sure she was waiting outside for a lift?" Tony asked us determinedly, as if we had gotten some small detail wrong.

"Yeah! Did you not see her? Oh no! Well perhaps it's for the best!" We both replied.

He explained how he had run through the lobby looking for her, she wasn't there. He thought she had gone because he was too slow. He thought he had let her down, dejectedly he went back inside his room.

This revelation only made Mark and I laugh even more as we rolled on the floor outside his room for at least another half an hour.

I don't think we ever told him, somewhere he is closing his eyes thinking, "If only I was quicker!"

32. IT WAS MY IDEA

In insurance, we were constantly looking for new ways to market our policies ahead of the competition. Something to resonate with customers to make your product something they wanted as well as needed.

The year was 1988, I would always fall asleep thinking of the things I would be doing the next day. A version of that old Walt Disney mantra,

"If you visualise it, you will do it."

One night at 2 a.m. I woke up, sat bolt upright, grabbed a pen and piece of paper and wrote down 2000.

I went into work the next day all excited. I had a brilliant idea to sell more policies. I grabbed my boss, and we went out to see some customers, armed with the question,

"How would you like £2000 so that you could celebrate the year 2000 anywhere you want on the planet or have the biggest street party ever?"

The biggest event of our lifetime was just over ten years away, a whole new century was about to begin.

By simply paying £10 a month, (£2.50 a week) into a ten-year endowment plan you would be insured and when the plan matured in 1999 you would have some spending money to do anything you wanted to celebrate the year 2000. How cool is that!

My boss loved it and more importantly customers loved it too.

Now, here's a lesson in why when you think of something, not only should you patent or copyright your ideas, but you should never ever share them with anyone until you have worked out any kind of fiscal reward.

Unfortunately, just as we were having some success, I went out sick for two weeks. When I walked back into the office, many folks were a little sheepish around me.

The company, a major global insurance company, had not only heard about my idea, but they had also created a new policy called "Policy 2000" and were in the process of printing new policy packaging, advertising, stationery, and customer handouts.

"Oh great!" I thought, fame at last, "there's bound to be a statue of me in the corridor soon."

Unbeknownst to me while I was off work my ideas had been shared. One of the group managers shared it in a conference speech, taking credit for it, and the company loved it so much they ran with it.

The whole thing became even more bizarre when I saw other insurance companies copy it and advertising similar campaigns in the national press, but it was "my idea" ha-ha.

33. **FULL COVERAGE**

A new customer, The Dator family moved into the streets I covered.

The lad who transferred the account to me used to laugh about how "glamourous" Mrs. Dator wasn't and tell the rest of the lads in the pub, how much of a shock I was in for when I went collecting the premiums.

Turns out that the lady of the house was very friendly and looked like she was in the movies. Okay the movie in question might have been Predator, but she was still a lovely lady.

We got along very well and even at one point I tried to arrange to help with the purchase of their home, which would have been a mortgage feather in my cap.

Whenever I walked in, Mrs. Dator would always ask me,

"Would you like a cup of tea, pet?"

Nothing unusual in her saying that, and of course I was always delighted to take a break and have a cup of tea and a cigarette, halfway round my collecting on a Friday afternoon.

The rest of the lads would always make fun of this, mainly because she was such a scary looker, but when you looked beyond the fearsome facial features, Mrs. Dator also had a lovely body. I used this to wind the others up and would jokingly tell them stories about how sexy she really was, then my favourite story to tell in the pub began on a Friday afternoon, and boy would they lap it up.

I was in Mrs. Dators house on my usual Friday stop, she stood beside me looking at my ledger entries. She was pretending to see if they all matched the entries in her log book, and I was pretending to cross reference with her.

Doing this she stood very close to me, pressing herself into me, and instead of moving away I pressed back against her very gently, mainly with my left arm and left leg.

After a few minutes, she exclaimed,

"What are you doing?"

"Oh, so sorry!" I said as I stepped away.

"Ha-ha!" She laughed and said, "Gotcha!"

"Oh ha-ha, yes you got me ha-ha!" I replied happy that I hadn't made a faux pas.

Then she shocked me as she said, "If that's what you want, you should come round on Monday after lunch when we have more time, and you can bring some of that mortgage information as an excuse."

"Oh, right, right, then I will do that, I'll be over about 1:30 pm." I replied quite bewildered at what was happening and what exactly I was agreeing to.

On Monday, I showed up at 1:25 pm. I was definitely more punctual than in my younger years.

I knocked and walked in, the kitchen was empty, and she was sitting on the sofa in the front room, which I could see once I was halfway through the kitchen.

"Hello." "I said, "I brought that mortgage stuff for you to look at. Is everyone home?"

"No just me." She said, then she nonchalantly turned back to watching the television.

I remembered the theme tune from "Neighbours" just starting. I walked back to the back door and turned the key to lock the door. The last thing I wanted was anyone else walking in, I felt really nervous as I walked into the front room and sat where her feet were on the sofa.

She was sitting at the far end of the sofa, with her legs curled up the way women do, so they're only occupying one cushion but they look all comfy and relaxed.

I reached my hand out and put it in her knee.

"What are you doing?" She exclaimed.

All I could think was, "Oh no! Is this another gotcha? Had I read the whole thing wrong? Was I mistaken?"

"Sorry!" I said out loud, "I thought that's what you wanted. My mistake, sorry about that. Erm here I have that mortgage information for you, and to make it more accurate I need some extra information."

"Oh good." She said, "What information do you need?"

I read from the list and she stood up and walked behind the small bar to get a box of papers.

"Is this the information?" She asked.

"That's some of it." I replied.

"Hang on." She said, and she disappeared into a cupboard under the stairs.

I saw her reach up and grab another box of papers.

"Here you go." She said as she handed me the few bits of paper I needed.

"Oh that's great!" I said, "We should celebrate, with a special cup of tea ha-ha!" I said as I squeezed her hand in mine, thinking she would feel a little more randy back in the kitchen like she did on Friday.

"Wait till I put this away." She said carrying the small box back into the unlit cupboard under the stairs.

She went into the cupboard and I saw her stretching.

"Well don't just stand there, come n help me!" She exclaimed.

"Oh right!" I said, putting the mortgage papers down and walking into the dark cupboard.

There was only enough room in the cupboard to squash four people inside in a game of hide and seek, she was facing me as I stepped in.

"Where does it go?" I asked.

"Oh you'll easy see where it goes ha-ha! But the box goes up there on that shelf." She raised her right arm to point at the high shelf to my left.

I took the box in my left hand and still facing her, I reached up, popping it back into the gap she had taken it from.

As my arm came down, she reached forward and kissed me.

With one box on the shelf, and another one in front of me, all I could hear her say was,

"Hang on, I'm not that tall!"

34. WHAT NOW?

I've always been lucky. Sure, things have gone wrong, but always something else comes along and a new direction moves me forward on to better things. Almost as if I had a guardian angel.

This time, a lad I'd been to school with who also worked in insurance, offered me a job.

My last job was gone because the coal mines were closing, They say don't believe your own publicity, and you shouldn't, but I will say that anyone who can make a living in the financial services industry in coal mining villages and be in the top three of a regional competition as the coal mines are closing, must be good at something.

He was a successful man. To illustrate his success he drove a Jaguar, I couldn't afford a Jaguar, he definitely had the more successful image in the financial services industry, and I didn't.

He employed me without an interview, which in my world is real plus, no chance of making goofy statements or sleeping in ha-ha.

The trouble was it was a commission only position, and when I tell you that "Anyone can get a commission only job, then I literally mean, anyone!"

I went to the office and set up ten appointments for the next two weeks. Everyone was impressed, setting appointments is easy. Setting meaningful and qualified appointments that a sale will result from is the difficult task.

I was provided with a list of existing customers, so I simply started dialling and would ask the customers who already had a policy,

"If they were still happy with the choice they made?"

If they said, "No!" Simply ask, "Why not?" Then arrange a visit to discuss how you can fix what they dislike.

If they say, "Yes!" Then thank them and let them know you have additional benefits to share with them.

Sometimes it was also easy to call and just to ask,

"When is a good time to visit and review everything?

Customers are thrilled that you're taking an interest.

Despite being able to set the appointments, I didn't work well in the scripted call structures being imposed on me. I had always worked like "The Sundance Kid" in the movie "Butch Cassidy and the Sundance Kid" starring Paul Newman and Robert Redford. There's a part where the miner asks The Sundance Kid to show how fast and good he is with a gun by shooting at a stone. Sundance Kid barely scratches the stone, but then asks, "Can I move?" And once he can "move" he really blasts that stone to pieces. That's how I function, if I can move and do my stuff, I'm usually on fire, that's because I'd built my own structure to follow and it worked for me.

In this position I had to follow their rules, fair enough they were successful, but the process felt just a little mercenary to me.

After a week or two, I just didn't see any future in it, so I stopped doing anything.

The lad who hired me asked that we should meet. I knew he was going to fire me; I'd never been fired but knew all the signs were there. I turned up to the meeting with a new haircut and suit.

In exactly the same way an expensive car makes some people think you are successful, then so does a shiny new suit and a haircut. Despite people claiming differently appearances and first impressions count.

I deliberately set out to use first impressions to disarm him. It worked. He changed his mind, and now the conversation turned to what he could do to help me. I listened and he was excited about the future, though I'm convinced we both knew I wouldn't be producing anything. We went through the motions, finished our meeting, finished our beers, and I never saw him again.

I have often asked myself,

"Why do people do these jobs?"

Great question! Looking back, I always thought I was so great, I could sell anything and make money anywhere. I'm being unkind to myself and others, there was certainly a time when the working person and home owner welcomed sales advisors into his or her home for a variety of different products, I was just in an industry that was destined to change forever, and I was the dinosaur.

I don't want to appear ungrateful; I do thank him for taking the chance on me. The trouble was even though I had been a good salesman, I really needed a job with a salary and structure. In hindsight I should have declined his offer and moved to a large city, somewhere completely different, or go and grab an education to further my career.

Lucky? Yeah I was then and I still am now.

35. HITTING THE SMALL TIME

I got a job in a small office, ridiculously small, two desks and three chairs made it full.

You could tell the two blokes, Derek and Bill, didn't really like each other, and on day one I'm already thinking.

"Wow this is great!"

Even worse, They each had a desk and I got the chair.

I knew some people frowned on these fellas, citing lack of professionalism in the way they approached their business, but at least I had a job, and at that time, I needed a job.

Derek and Bill were both about fifteen years older than me, how they got through each day I'll never know. Both smoked like a pair of industrial chimneys, ashtrays on their desks were always heaped high, with tab ash and tab butts piled on top of each other like some smoker's smelly Jenga game.

They both liked a drink, but thankfully, they never brought that into the office, instead, Bill would disappear early each afternoon and never return, whilst Derek would disappear at 11 am and sometimes come back at 5 pm after a "long lunch" and sometimes never came back. This usually left me "in charge" most afternoons.

Not sure how I lasted there eight months, but I did. No computer, and after the first month, once they figured out I could do their work and mine, I didn't see much of either of them.

One afternoon, during my first month, a time when they would both be sitting there fidgety, all ants in their pants looking for excuses not to be there, Bill was sitting at his desk and you could see he was looking especially uncomfortable.

Derek asked him

"What's up with you there partner?"

"Not sure!" Replied Bill, "I have pains in my left arm! And they feel like they're running up my shoulder!

Derek and I looked at each other, slightly worried.

"Are you having a heart attack?" I asked.

"Should we call you an ambulance?" Asked Derek.

It must have been bad because they both stubbed out their cigarettes. Then they pulled those faces middle aged men pull when worrying over their mortality.

Derek and I got out of our chairs and walked over to Bill's desk.

"It might be quicker if we take him in the car!" Said Derek, talking to me as if we were debating some surgical procedure where the patient couldn't hear us.

Bill wasn't saying much, so we stood on each side of him thinking we would at least help him to his feet and get him to the car, I'm still not sure that's a good thing for a heart attack patient. Bill grimaced as we grabbed his arms, and let out and audible,

"Ow!!" As Derek took hold of his left arm.

Derek started laughing. Bill was still making painful noises; I was looking confused.

"Argh! That's right where it hurts!" Said Bill as Derek gripped his left arm and raised it even higher.

"Ha-ha! You fucking numpty!" Laughed Derek.

"What!" Complained Bill, "I'm in agony man!"

Derek continued through his laughter,

"It's drawing pins stuck in your arm, yer great tattie!"

Just then the drawing pins started falling out of the elbow of the jacket Bill was wearing, plinking onto the desk in front of all three of us. He had been sitting with his elbows on the desk, and he had plonked his left elbow straight into a pile of drawing pins. You couldn't have made it up.

Oh, for the world of phone cameras, I'm sure that would have gone viral.

It wasn't long before Bill didn't even bother coming into the office and I gained a desk.

36. DRINK UP

Me, Derek and Bill, went to a manufacturing facility to view new products. Remember Hawick, (pronounced hoy k, not Hay wick) I was returning to the scene of an earlier story. Once again there would be an overnight stay. At least this time I packed an overnight bag for the trip.

We had three rooms all booked next to each other, and not having to drive home the same day, made it easy for the three of us just to sit in the bar of the Scottish hotel until the wee hours of the morning.

The great thing about the bar in a hotel is that it's only closing time when your mouth can no longer utter any words that the barman can understand. For an Englishman in a Scottish bar, that is indeed a rarity, given that he can understand drunk Scottish folks, understanding us was never going to be a challenge.

By the time we decided it was bedtime and our legs were full, Bill could hardly walk and any coherent conversation was now several hours behind us.

We all stood to go to our rooms, and as if to demonstrate to the barman that he had indeed served us plenty of good alcohol, Bill leaned forward, and nose planted himself on the table in front of us. Derek and I burst out laughing. We were never in agreement about whether the barman was saying,

"Dinnit worry lads, I've seen this all before!" Or "You dozy Sassenach bastards, makin a mess, get the hell outta my sight!"

Me and Derek each took an arm of Bill, he wasn't a lightweight, okay I'm being kind, he was fat, and together as we stumbled towards our rooms, we made more noise than a herd of wildebeest thundering through the corridors.

We made it to his door, and Bill suddenly decided he would walk in on his own.

"Am areet man, ah can dee it, leave iz alern!" Were his protests as we stood outside his room.

There was no way he was going to allow us into his room. To this day I still have no idea what on earth he could have had in his room that was so precious, but he was adamant that we open his door and leave him.

"Fuck off man, yers, are not comin in me fuckin room man!"

Derek and I didn't want a commotion in the hallway in the wee hours of the morning, and we just laughed, shaking our heads and said,

"Fine, don't worry, we winnit come in your precious room!"

He somehow managed in all of this to shove his hand in his pocket and fish out his room key card, this was a good thing, because neither Derek nor I fancied trying to stick our hands in his pockets. In typical drunk fashion there was no way he could find the lock to slide it through.

After several failed and frustrated attempts, Derek took his key card and opened his door, handed him his key back, pointed him into the doorway and pushed him forward through the door, with the words,

"Goodnight! See ya in the morning!"

Bill stumbled through the open doorway and into the darkness of his room. The door closed on its spring, and just as we turned to go to our own rooms, there was the mightiest clattering and banging from inside his room. As if someone had fallen through the roof. Derek and I looked at each other horrified, partly because we wondered if the shove we had given him was a fatal shove, and partly because we thought the extra noise must surely wake every other guest in the hotel, and possibly even disturb the management.

Immediately, we banged on his bedroom door, we heard from the other side of the door movement, at least we knew he wasn't dead. After a few seconds and some shuffling from the other side of the door, Bill opened the door, looking very sheepish.

"What?" He asked with an impish grin.

"That fuckin noise!" Hissed Derek in a loud whisper. "What was that? Are you alright?"

"Am alright man!" Hissed Bill back from his doorway. "I just put the lights on and thowt there was another bloke in me room! So I went ter clobber the bastad!"

"What?" Hissed Derek incredulously, "You did what?"

By now I had started to have a fit of the giggles, caused by way too much drink and stupidity going on in my universe.

"Oh my God! Can you believe this bloke!" Derek turned to me laughing, "He's just gone and put the light on and started a fight with his reflection in the closet mirror."

In the hallway of his room was a full floor to ceiling mirror, he had seen himself in the full mirror then attacked his own reflection. Luckily, there was no damage to the mirror or himself, that was the night he invented "Fight Club!"

Bill closed his door, and we headed to our rooms. Derek was paranoid about sleeping in and asked me to take his spare room key and wake him up in the morning when it was time to leave, now only a matter of hours away.

A few hours later, I used Derek's room key to go in and wake him up. He was snoring. The thing that struck me most was that he had decided to pack before he went to sleep, obviously looking for a quick exit when he woke up. I was sure we'd already paid the bill so I had no clue why we needed to bolt quickly.

I couldn't help giggling as I quietly opened his bags and started to put things from his room into his luggage, basically anything that wasn't nailed down, towels, soap and even the bedside hotel telephone into his overnight bag.

I was giggling so much to myself that I had to leave and come back. When I later went back to his room, I pretended it was my first-time walking in and made a lot of noise to wake him up. I saw that he stirred awake, then I was off to my room to wait until they both wanted to leave.

Halfway home, about an hour down the road, we stopped for coffee and breakfast.

While we were walking in I started laughing.

"What's up with you, you're acting like a loony!" Said Derek.

"Yeah!" Said Bill, "Give over laughing, or all the people inside are gonna be saying, 'look at those two nice blokes taking out that special needs fella for breakfast, ah! And they've purra nice suit on him anarl"

That made me laugh louder and harder, and still laughing I said, "Okay, okay, I've got to tell ya! Ha-ha! When we get back to the office if the hotel calls, you'd berra ignore the call ha-ha! Especially if they're suggesting that you stole things from the room."

Now Derek laughed out loud and said

"Oh aye!" I noticed that before we left, so I put it all in Bill's bag in case we were stopped on the way out!"

"Yer did what?" Shouted Bill, as we all walked into the breakfast place rolling around laughing at the stupidity of the last twenty-four hours.

37. THAT'S SELLING ALRIGHT?

Despite my misgivings, selling things can be fun. One salesman had a problem with drinking too much. In order that he didn't drink and drive, the company we worked for paid for a driver for him.

The trouble was, he would still have a drink before going to an appointment to "calm his nerves."

One time he sank four cans of lager and four cans of cider while waiting to go in one house and was only in the house fifteen minutes before he came back out, the biggest problem was he'd spent ten of the fifteen minutes in the customers bathroom, and not for a number one.

Another bloke used to walk in and begin bartering the price immediately. He would usually start the conversation asking if they were prepared to pay forty quid a month, but if they couldn't pay forty then he could help sort them for thirty, and if they couldn't then what was the maximum they would pay? I asked him how he never got thrown out, he said they appreciated his directness.

Once I walked into a house to meet a noticeably young couple and decided I should spend some time building rapport. While we were chit chatting, we stood near the window and were looking out at the neighbourhood,

"Nice area round here." I was remarking.

"Yeah we like it." Was their unremarkable response, which is a good thing, because now we were agreeing about things which subconsciously are supposed to work in my favour.

Then I pointed to a beaten up little old Austin Mini car you could just see on the corner of the street, worth around £150, and said,

"Ha-ha! It's a good job there's not many like that round here!"

Yup, it was their car.

I walked into one house where the gentleman sat at the dining table with me, away from his wife. His wife wasn't interested, she sat in the lounge area, not taking her eyes off the soap on TV. This was never a good sign.

The gentleman pulled out a big piece of paper, I could see lots of numbers and writing on it. Smiling, I asked,

"Is that a list of your requirements? If so, that's a good place to start."

"Oh no!" He replied, "This is the ten other prices I've already been quoted!"

I smiled and rose to leave, saying,

"In that case, I won't waste any more of your time, thank you for the invite, just call me when you're ready to proceed!"

He was quite shocked, open mouthed, he spurted out, "What about my quote?"

"You already have plenty of quotes." I replied. "I hardly think another one is of any use or even needed. Do you mind if I take a look at those?"

He proudly handed me the list. I quickly looked down his list of quotes, smiled and said,

"Well, we're cheaper than some and more expensive than others! Better than some and as good as the others."

Then I continued, "I'm particularly good at what I do, and I'm sure that out of these ten, one or two would be as good as I am. If you didn't buy from any of them, I don't think you would buy from me!" And with that I took my leave.

Sometimes the reverse is true as well, I once got to an appointment and the gentleman opened the door and said,

"I don't care what you have or how much it costs; We don't want any!"

I smiled and replied, "Well thank you for letting me know in advance, that saves us a lot of time. However, I wonder what made you make the appointment? I have travelled an hour to be here. Before I turn around and go back, is it possible to have a cup of tea?"

We sat down with a cup of tea, talked about the weather, how long he'd lived there, and other small talk then after ten minutes he asked,

"So what is the main thing you do?"

"Oh!" I said, "Let me give you the quick version."

I promptly gave him a five-minute run through of real people I knew who had benefited from the product.

As soon as I finished, he said,

"Hang on!"

He left me alone in the kitchen for five minutes and went into the next room. When he returned he brought his cheque book with him and wrote out a check to purchase the product in full.

To change the song lyrics of one of my favourite TV shows "Auf Wiedersehen Pet," That's selling alright.

38. RAM RAID

I had an appointment in a rundown part of town. The violence and drugs in that area were so bad that if you had bought a property there, you would have trouble selling or even renting it. I knew it didn't look good as I got near but I wasn't too worried as it was noon and broad daylight.

I pulled up outside the house and parked in front, opposite a field leading up to some high-rise apartments. The other side of the field had concrete poles erected to prevent vehicles driving across the green area.

The man opened the door and let me in. As we stepped in, he said,

"We can talk in here!" As he pointed to the kitchen on my left.

I didn't mind where we were so long as he was comfortable. Then he said, "Yeah, we can stand here and keep an eye on your car out of the kitchen window."

I must have looked curious because he followed up with, "Yeah they see a strangers car round here and they're likely to want to try stealing it!"

"Oh!" I said, "That's strange, it's daylight and I'm at your house."

"Yeah," he continued, "That doesn't matter, the police won't come in here, and they usually just drive the car until it's a wreck."

He had just finished explaining all of this when a car went screaming across the grass in front of us. The car stopped at the other side of the field in front of the concrete bollards. Maybe they were just going to abandon it or come back this way to the road. After about thirty seconds, there was a crowd of people gathered of all ages.

The car reversed about twenty feet, and spun around so now it was facing us, then reversed as fast as it could, going the other way and slamming into the concrete poles on the other side of the field. My jaw dropped,

"Oh my goodness!" I exclaimed, "What the heck are they doing?"

You could see the crowd of people, many adults among the throng of kids, cheering the driver on, as he eased the car forward again, getting ready to reverse back into the poles.

"They're going to ram out the middle concrete poles." Explained my host, "They knock them out now. Then tonight, if the police cars chase them, they can drive right through where the poles used to be and round the estate without restriction!"

"Wow!" I said, stood there with my jaw still dropping, and asked, "Shouldn't we call the police?"

"Oh no! Never!" My host explained with a look of horror on his face. "They would know that somebody snitched, and the consequences wouldn't be good!"

Watching this unfold in front of my own eyes, knowing nobody will believe this, looking out of the window, I realized that these folks weren't the types of folks to be reasoned with.

I was driving a Volvo. Those of you who know cars, will know that a Volvo came with the reputation as the safest vehicle on the road, built with an inner steel cage frame, which not only would knock out the poles but also the apartment block behind them as well.

My host clearly couldn't defend me or my vehicle, the police wouldn't come to rescue me, I made the executive decision to leave. I said to my host,

"Thank you for inviting me! I'm deeply sorry the company won't be able to provide you with a suitable bid for the job! Goodbye!"

And with that I left post haste. Not only did the job not pay that well, but I certainly wasn't being paid enough to stand and try to deter a bunch of folks who would ram raid bollards in the street, and I could certainly never send a work crew through to work there. Imagine ha-ha! After half an hour on the job all of their tools and van would have been swiped from under them.

39. WILD CALL

Working in a call centre is usually described as being soulless, dull, or monotonous. Any words you care to think of to make it not sound fun, that was not the case when I was working there.

If we were working the later shift, we were encouraged to have a glass of wine or beer, and pizza. Straight away people would be happier and crucially, it puts that all important smile on the employees face to answer each call in a happy, positive mood. Or alternatively we were just a bunch of drunk pizza lovers let loose with the company phone system.

We would laugh at many things, people on opposite units provocatively eating a banana while you're trying to focus. Others tried to unplug your screen when you were in the middle of a quote, and our favourite, when Michele would walk in from the cold and we could immediately see just how cold she was due to the protuberance through her blouse and bra.

I remember one call, a lady we'll call Fiona, looking for a cheaper quotation than the one her existing company had provided her with. Fiona was flirting on the phone, and of course I was flirting back. I gave her the price, and without hesitation, the first words out of her mouth were,

"Fuck! That's too much!"

Nobody had ever sworn at me and that resonated with me. Fiona asked me to call her back later if an improvement could be found to the price. I told her that was unlikely, but I could call her later to confirm if that was okay with her. Fiona agreed.

There I was working in a call centre, all my calls recorded for the boss to hear if she wanted and I'd practically just arranged to call a customer later on, yeah okay not practically, I had just arranged to call a customer later on. I made the return call on a non-recorded line; it was my cell phone. We arranged to meet in a pub where Fiona would be working, about forty miles away, or an hour in the car.

I'd never been one for blind dates, I had never even been on one. I finished work and raced home, got changed, put my cheap aftershave on and set out for my blind date. Fiona felt comfortable meeting me in the pub where she worked. That way if it turned out we weren't getting along; Fiona didn't have far to go and be with a load of friends.

I got there just after 8 pm. A beautiful country pub, the kind you see on a British tourist board advertisement. I called her from outside to make sure she was there. I got out of the car, puffed out my now considerable forty-two-inch chest and walked in the door at the rear of the pub, through a small corridor and into the bar.

There was Fiona to greet me, but this wasn't at all like The Green Green Grass of Home, more like the Monster Mash. The bar was full of rugby players, let me be clear, there's absolutely nothing wrong with rugby players, especially on a rugby field, it's just that, well let me use her words.

Fiona - "Oh! I thought you would be bigger!" (Giggles)

Me - "Oh! And I thought you would be smaller!" (laughs)

Fiona - "Well I don't think it's going to work; my ex-husband was six foot five inches and weighed 152 kilos' (334 lbs.). He loved to play rugby and was very athletic."

Me - "Oh! And I thought you'd be smaller!

As Fiona continued to explain our incompatibility, which needed absolutely no explanation whatsoever, I decided to have a beer. Which I ended up drinking on my own.

Fiona disappeared quicker than Milli Vanilli's career, presumably to mingle in a different part of the bar. This was her local so I'm sure the regulars must have all fell on the floor laughing as soon as I left. Asking Fiona where her new pet Oompa Loompa had gone to?

The part that you can't see from her words is that, in Fiona's last relationship, the ex-husband wasn't the biggest or toughest one in the family, that would have been her, and there I stood six feet tall in my nicely pressed t-shirt and jeans standing about six inches shorter than Fiona and weighing a whole human being less than her, about the only way she would find me attractive would have been as a snack.

I just wasn't going to measure up to be the kind of man she would be with. Just goes to show how misleading we all sound on the phone to a stranger. Clearly on future phone calls I needed to stop doing Arnold Schwarzenegger impressions.

With that I left the bar, the job, the country and boarded a plane deciding to head out west to Texas.

If you made it this far, thank you, and if you didn't, then you won't see this until the movie comes out. Part two (coming soon) sees our intrepid hero come to America.

This wasn't a bad first little book, and taken in the spirit for which it was intended I hope you found it enjoyable, a few short funny, silly stories I remembered from bygone years; however I would like to point out…

I have tried to recreate events, locales and conversations from my memories of them. In order to maintain their anonymity in some instances I have changed the names of individuals and places, I may have changed some identifying characteristics and details such as physical properties, occupations, and places of residence. Any similarity to persons real or fictitious is purely coincidental.

© 2022, Ben Teeley

ABOUT THE AUTHOR

Aged fifteen, I stumbled out of the school gates for the last time, suddenly realizing I wasn't required to go to school anymore. There was no fanfare, no graduation party, nobody said goodbye, I just went home and was expected to find a job. This wasn't unusual at the time for me or my friends, we just never seemed to draw lines under these things.

Born into a large family in industrial north east England, I started working when I was aged sixteen. Straight away I loved this first job so much I would often work twelve-hour days, doing so much extra work, that the first shift the next morning had nothing to do until lunchtime.

Always hard working, living by that old adage. 'work hard and play hard.'

I continued working in retail, then insurance, always looking for the humour at work, especially in the people.

From bomb experts to blind dates, it's all here.

A keen Sunderland AFC supporter, I also enjoy music, pets and homelife.

I've tried to capture some of those moments in this collection of funny stories, as I stumbled from one career to the next.

Starting with my very first interview, book one takes you through funny, touching, and tragic work stories before I uproot and head west to America.

BONUS MATERIAL

This is written in English UK spelling and meanings as opposed to the USA. If google isn't helpful to my transatlantic readers maybe the list below will help clear some words up. I have tried to list them in order of appearance, apologies if I missed some.

UK	**USA**
Bloke	Man
Holiday	Vacation
Skip	Dumpster
Lorry	18-Wheeler
Tab	Cigarette
Estate Car	Station Wagon
Mincemeat	Ground Beef
Coppers	Policeman
Pissed	Drunk
Take the piss	Make fun of
Stone	14lbs
1 Kilo	2.2lbs

Friends

Some people say, "Good friends are hard to find!" In this respect I must be the richest person alive. I have had some of the best friends a person could wish for, the kind you call anytime, any day or night, they never are annoyed, they just want to help. Tragically over the years, I've also had to say goodbye to some of the best friends a person could wish for. For the inspiration, our times together, the memories and the laughs each of you shared, thank you, I dedicate this book to the memory of Keith, Alan, Dez and Barry.

And to my friends still out there, thank you, stay safe!

Picture Below: Fancy dress was always a winner at work.

PODCAST

Stay tuned, I will be launching a podcast, Teeley's Top Tales, or Tea With a Teeley, depending which acronym you think would be best. Or maybe an audio book, these will include some stories which never made the written version but deserve a telling.

Thank you so much, I appreciate you taking the time to read and enjoy my little book.

If indeed you enjoyed reading, please consider giving it a review on Amazon.

© 2022, Ben Teeley

Printed in Great Britain
by Amazon